People Like That

BY THE SAME AUTHOR

GENTLEMEN OF THE WEST
LEAN TALES
(WITH JAMES KELMAN AND ALASDAIR GRAY)
LIKE BIRDS IN THE WILDERNESS
A WORKING MOTHER

People Like That

Agnes Owens

BLOOMSBURY

First published 1996
Copyright © 1996 by Agnes Owens
The moral right of the author
has been asserted

Bloomsbury Publishing Plc, 2 Soho Square, London W1V 6HB

A CIP catalogue record for this book
is available from the British Library

10 9 8 7 6 5 4 3 2 1

ISBN 0 7475 2522 6

Typeset by Hewer Text Composition Services, Edinburgh
Printed in Great Britain by Clays Ltd, St Ives plc

Lines from 'South of the Border' by Jimmy
Kennedy and Michael Carr © 1939 renewed
by The Peter Maurice Music Co. Ltd, London.
Sole selling agents: Shapiro, Bernstein and Co. Inc.,
New York.

ACKNOWLEDGEMENTS

The following stories have been published previously:

'The Lighthouse' in *Chapman 4* (The Women's Forum),
  1993.
'The Collectors' in *Tales from the Coast: Stories from West
  Coast Magazine*, Taranis Books, 1991.
'The Warehouse' in *Undercover: an anthology of Scottish
  writing*, Mainstream Publishing, 1993.
'When Shankland Comes' in *The Seven Deadly Sins*,
  Serpent's Tail, 1988.
'People Like That' in *West Coast Magazine*, Issue 13,
  1992.
'The Castle' in *The Seven Cardinal Virtues*, Serpent's
  Tail, 1990.
'Marching to the Highlands and Into the Unknown' in the
  Guardian, 1985.

CONTENTS

THE LIGHTHOUSE

'Let's go somewhere else,' said Megan to her brother Bobby playing on the beach with his pail and spade. 'Let's go to the lighthouse.'

'I don't want to,' he said, without looking up. At three and a half years he had the face of an angel, but his appearance belied a strong determination to have everything his own way. So thought Megan, aged ten.

'You can stay if you like,' she said, 'but I'm going and I just hope a monster doesn't get you.'

At the mention of the word 'monster' he began to look over his shoulder. It was only recently she'd been telling him about monsters and how they ate children. She'd even shown him a picture of one in an animal book, which was actually that of a gorilla, but it had been enough to make him refuse to sleep with the light off and even with it on he would waken up screaming.

'I don't want to go to the lighthouse,' he said, running over and butting her in the stomach with his head.

'But I do,' she said, skipping off lightly over the sand.

'Wait for me,' he called, picking up his pail and spade and trailing after her.

Together they walked along in a friendly way, going at a pace that suited them both. The day was warm but with a bit of wind. Megan almost felt happy. They came to a part of the shore that was deserted except for a woman walking her dog in the distance. Bobby stopped to gather shells.

'Throw them away,' said Megan. 'You'll get better ones at the lighthouse.'

He emptied his pail then asked if the lighthouse was over there, pointing to the sea wall.

'Don't be stupid. The lighthouse is miles away.'

He said emphatically, 'Then I don't want to go.'

Megan lost her temper. 'If you don't start moving I'll slap your face.'

At that moment the woman with the dog passed by. 'Is that big girl hitting you?' she asked him.

Before he could speak, Megan had burst out, 'He's my brother and I'll hit him if I want.'

The woman studied them through thoughtful, narrowed eyes. 'Do your parents know you're out here in this lonely place?'

When Megan said they did the woman walked on with the dog, muttering something under her breath which Megan suspected was some kind of threat aimed at her. She hissed to Bobby, 'See what you've done. For all we know she could be going to report us to the police and you know what that means?'

'What?'

'Mummy and Daddy will be put in jail for neglecting us and I'll have to watch you for ever.'

At that he let out a howl so loud she was forced to put her hand over his mouth.

'Be quiet, you fool. Do you want that woman back?' He quietened down when she promised to get him an ice-cream.

'Where's the van?' he asked, looking around.

'Over there,' she said, pointing in the direction of the lighthouse. At first he believed this, running beside her eagerly, but when they went on for a considerable length without any signs of an ice-cream van he began to lag behind.

'Come on,' she said, 'or we'll miss it.'

'Where is it?'

'Don't ask me stupid questions,' she snapped, thinking how it wasn't fair that she had to be saddled with him all the time. 'You're a silly bugger anyway.'

'I'm telling you swore.'

'Tell if you want,' said Megan, thinking her parents couldn't say much considering the way they swore.

'If you don't come – ' she began, when he started walking again, and just when she thought he was going to act reasonably for once he stopped in front of a rock.

'Look! There are fish in there,' he said.

Grumbling, she went back to investigate. It was true. There were tiny fish darting about a pool of water within a crevice in the rock.

'Aren't they pretty?' she said, just as he threw a stone into the pool causing them to disappear. She shook him by the shoulders.

'You have to spoil everything, don't you?' she said, letting him go suddenly so that he sat down with a thud. But he was up on his feet quick enough when she said, walking backwards, 'A monster's going to get you one of these days, the way you carry on.'

After a good deal of tramping over dry sand that got into their shoes and made their feet sore, Megan suggested they climb up over the dunes on their right-hand side to see if there was a better and quicker path that would take them to the lighthouse. He didn't answer. She suspected he was still brooding about the ice-cream, but he followed her which was the main thing.

Climbing the sand dunes wasn't easy. They kept sliding back down. Bobby did it deliberately thinking it was funny. Megan was glad to see him in a better mood. When they got to the top they found they were on a golf course stretching for miles with nobody on it but a man in a grey track suit. He saw them, came over and said, 'Better watch out you don't get hit with a golf ball. It's not safe up here.'

Megan asked him if he was a golfer – she noticed he wasn't carrying any clubs. When he told her he was just out for the day collecting golf balls, she began to wonder if he might be one of those strangers they'd been warned not to speak to.

'Bobby,' she said loudly, 'we'd better go back. Mummy and Daddy will be looking for us.'

'But I thought – ' he began and was cut off by Megan pulling him back down the sandy slope. When he got to the bottom he said that he'd wanted to stay up there.

'It's not safe,' she said.

'Why not?' Then, as if it had nothing to do with anything, he let out a tremendous wail.

'In the name of God, what is it now,' she said, in the same tone her mother used when totally exasperated.

'I've left my pail and spade,' he said, pointing up at the sand dunes.

She felt like strangling him. 'Well, I'm not going for them,' but when he began to wail loud enough to split the rocks, she said she would go if he came with her to the lighthouse.

'I don't want to,' he said, stamping his feet in temper. 'I want to go back to that other beach where Mummy left us.'

It was then she decided she'd had enough of his tantrums. 'Go then,' she said, giving him a shove so that he tottered on blindly for a few steps. 'I don't want to ever see you again.'

When he turned round she was racing along the beach at a fair speed. He called on her to come back, though it was doubtful she heard him above the cries of the seagulls, but even if she had, she probably wouldn't have stopped anyway.

On arriving at the lighthouse, she saw there was no way to get close to it as it was surrounded by water, not unless she waited until the tide went out and that would take hours. Sullenly, she looked up at its round turreted shape thinking it was much more boring from this angle than it had seemed from a distance. She wished she'd never come. The sea was stormy now with the waves lashing over the rocks. The whole venture had been a complete waste of time and energy, she decided. Suddenly her attention was riveted to what looked like a body in the water. For a split second she thought it was Bobby, which would have been quite impossible considering the distance she'd come. Nevertheless, it was a great relief to discover this was only a mooring buoy. She laughed at her mistake then began to feel uneasy. She could picture him stumbling into the sea for a paddle thinking it was all shallow water. It was the kind of stupid thing he was liable to do. Panic swept over her. What if something terrible happened to him? She should never have left him like that. Without another thought for the lighthouse or anything but Bobby, she began running back to where she'd left him, praying that he'd be all right.

From a distance she saw him hunkered down, digging in the sand. He must have gone up the sand dunes to get his pail and spade after all, she thought. She slowed down, her legs tired and aching, then to her dismay she saw the man they'd met on the golf course. He was hovering a few yards behind Bobby poking some debris on the shore with a stick.

'Bobby!' she called out sharply. 'Come over to me at once.'

He either didn't hear this or pretended not to, but the man did. He looked up at her and began to walk smartly in their direction. Galvanized into taking some kind of action, she ran forward to reach Bobby first. In fact she'd almost got to him when she slipped on a stone covered in seaweed and went down, the back of her head hitting off its sharp edge.

Her eyes were staring up at the sky as the man and Bobby crouched beside her. Bobby said, 'You shouldn't have left me. I'm telling Mummy.'

The man pulled him back. 'Leave her alone. She's in bad enough shape.' Then he put his lips close to her ear. 'Can you hear me?'

When her eyes flickered he put his hand over her mouth and nose and held it there for a considerable time. After that he turned to Bobby saying, 'We'll have to get an ambulance. You can come with me.'

Bobby said he didn't want to get an ambulance. He wanted to go back to the other beach.

'All right,' said the man, taking him by the hand and dragging him towards the sand dunes with Bobby protesting all the way. His cries died down when they vanished over the top.

Later that afternoon, a strong breeze sprang up along the shore, lifting clouds of sand into the air as well as the strands of Megan's hair drifting across her face. Seagulls came down to stand on her and poke her with their beaks, then, as if not liking what they found they flew off to the horizon whilst imperceptibly and gradually her body sank into the sand making a groove for itself. A passer-by might have thought she was asleep, she looked so peaceful. But no one came by that day and in the evening when the sun went down she was gone with the tide.

THE COLLECTORS

D avey came up over the steep, stony track that would lead him to the golf course once he had climbed a fence and crossed a burn. Sometimes he stopped to catch his breath. He was coming up for sixty and a hard life had taken its toll. When he reached the fence he became uneasy. Tam Duggan sat on a tree stump, arms folded as if patiently waiting on him.

'Saw ye comin' in the distance,' said Tam with a jovial smile. 'I thought I might as well go along wi' ye.'

'Aye,' said Davey with a nod. He could hardly refuse the offer for Tam was a big strong-looking fellow in his early twenties with a police record as long as his arm, mainly for assault.

He climbed stiffly over the fence then jumped the narrow burn with Tam following more easily.

'Up collectin' your golf ba's?' said Tam. 'I hear you dae quite well.'

'No' bad,' mumbled Davey, his voice lost in the

wind that had sprung up carrying a drizzle of rain with it.

He gave his companion a sidelong glance, wondering if he was as bad as folk said — it was easy to be in trouble nowadays, especially if you were young and had nothing to take up your time.

Tam faced him and said humbly, 'I hope you don't mind me comin' along wi' ye. I thought I might try some collectin' masel'.'

His coarse, handsome face was marred by a scar running the length of the left cheek.

'Why no'?' said Davey. 'It's a free country,' though his heart sank. He didn't want anyone else poaching, at least not alongside him. Others who collected golf balls were usually solitary figures in the distance, acting as if they were out for a stroll and keeping well clear of each other.

'It's right cauld up here,' said Tam, ducking his head from the wind and sticking his hands in the pockets of his flimsy black anorak.

'The higher you climb, the caulder it gets,' said Davey, himself warm enough under the thick cloth of a donkey jacket purchased from an ex-Youth Training Scheme employee.

He paused to pick up a golf ball a few inches off the path. Tam looked, round and said with surprise, 'You've got wan already and we're naewhere near the course?'

'Ye can get the odd wan as far doon as the fermer's field but up the tap beside the golf course is the best place.' The words were hardly out of Davey's mouth when Tam was bounding on ahead. 'I hope he stays oot ma road,' said Davey under his breath. Without hurrying he found two more golf balls on the way up. When he reached the top Tam was standing not far from the path, his face a picture of misery.

'Ma feet are soakin,' he said. 'It's a bog here.'

'Ah well,' said Davey, regarding his own heavy wellingtons complacently, 'you've got to put on the right gear for this business.'

'How was I tae know?' said Tam, staring ahead in a sullen manner at the long stretch of grass, moss and whin bushes parallel to the golf course.

'You can always go back,' said Davey.

'I might as well stay noo that I'm up here,' said Tam, walking on slowly. Then his long arm swooped down on the rough grass. 'A golf ba,' he shouted, 'a pure yellow wan tae. It's a beauty.'

Davey came up to join him.

'Very nice. A good make as well. You've done no' bad.'

'No' bad! I've done better than you. This is pure yellow and you've only got a white wan.'

'I've got three,' said Davey, tapping his pocket.

'Ye never telt me that,' said Tam, looking put out. 'How no'?'

'Dae I have tae tell ye everythin'?' said Davey, suddenly feeling fed up and wishing he had turned back when he first clapped eyes on this big pest. Abruptly he veered off through the moss down towards a drainage ditch where he immediately found two balls under the water. His pleasure was lost when Tam called, 'Don't tell me you've got anither wan.'

'Naw, two,' Davey called back, deciding that he was

going to try and ignore Tam's attitude as best he could for there was no point in getting worked up about it. The guy was worse than bad – he was mentally retarded. At the same time he was almost glad when five minutes later Tam found a ball within a clump of gorse, cursing the needles pricking his hand as he pulled it out.

'Anither wan,' he shouted, holding it up for Davey's inspection.

Thank God for that, thought Davey to himself. Being forced to study it he noticed it was chipped but said, 'Aye, very good,' with a false encouraging nod.

The wind died down and the rain became heavier. The view of the town below was blanked out with mist. Tam said to Davey, 'This weather would sicken ye.'

'Aye,' replied Davey, thinking it wasn't the only thing. He added, 'At least it keeps the golfers away.' So far he had seen only three on the other side of the course and they appeared to be hurrying in the direction of the clubhouse.

'Them!' said Tam contemptuously. 'They want their heids examined.'

By the time they were halfway along the edge of the course, Davey had found another three and Tam another one, which Davey had kicked in his direction when Tam wasn't looking, simply to keep his mouth shut. For a minute or two it did the trick, then he began to complain again.

'I'm soaked through.'

'There's a hut no' far away,' Davey told him. 'We'll take a bit shelter and see whit happens.'

Before they reached the hut Tam said in an urgent tone, 'Listen – how much dae ye get for golf ba's?'

'How much?' said Davey, frowning thoughtfully. 'Oh well, at the maist three for a pound.'

'Is that a'?' said Tam, looking offended. 'I heard ye got a pound each.'

'I don't know where ye heard that, but I've only ever got three for a pound.'

'So you're tellin' me,' said Tam, his voice heavy with sarcasm.

'As ye know yersel',' said Davey, trying to keep his temper, 'stolen property loses hauf its value by the time it reaches a buyer.'

'I bet I could get two quid for that yellow golf ba' any day,' said Tam. He snapped his fingers in the air. 'Jist like that.'

'You try it then,' said Davey, thankful to be nearing the hut. He would take a rest, drink the can of super lager he had in the back pocket of his trousers, then return home. He'd had enough of this fellow. They entered the hut and sat on a bench against the back wall – Tam gingerly on the edge of it, as it was exceedingly damp, and Davey leaning back carelessly with his legs stretched out.

'It's as cauld and wet in here than whit it is ootside,' said Tam.

Davey brought out his can of super lager. He offered it to Tam.

'Here, take a wee drap o' this. It might heat ye up.'

'No thanks,' said Tam, with a look of disgust. 'I cannae go that stuff. It tastes like gnats' piss.'

'Maybe so,' said Davey, 'but ye get accustomed tae the taste. Besides, it's the effect I'm efter.'

'Whit effect?' sneered Tam, staring moodily through the

wide-open doorway of the hut. 'I'd rather have a hauf bottle o' Bell's, or even a joint. Dae you know there's mair effect wi' a joint than that stuff.'

'I widnae know,' said Davey, putting the can to his mouth and wishing he had another two to go with it, for there really wasn't much effect from one can when he came to think of it.

'How many golf ba's did ye say ye had?' Tam suddenly asked.

'Er – eh, five,' said Davey vaguely.

'So, I've got three and that makes eight. If we got anither two that would be ten. I know where I could sell them for a pound each and that would be a fiver tae you and a fiver tae me.'

Davey took another pull at his can. Definitely there was no effect from it at all and there wouldn't likely to be with this blowhard rabbiting on in his ear.

'I'm gaun hame shortly,' he said. 'I don't feel sae good.'

'Haw – flyman,' jibed Tam.

This angered Davey. 'Whit dae ye mean – flyman? I'm gaun hame, and that's that.'

'Aye, because you've got the maist ba's, that's how.'

'So whit, if I have,' said Davey, beginning to feel a slight hit off the lager, which increased his anger. 'I found them, didn't I?'

'That's only because you were lucky. I wis lookin' every bit as hard as you and soaked tae the skin intae the bargain. Look at ma trainers. They're ruined.'

Davey continued to drink his lager while Tam paced up and down the mud floor of the hut, his face grim and determined. He stopped suddenly to point his forefinger at Davey's face.

'OK, if you're no' collectin' I want yer golf ba's.'

'You're no gettin' them,' said Davey, his voice less strong than he had intended as Tam leaned over him and growled, 'Haund them ower, pal.'

Davey's patience was broken. He flung the contents of his can straight at Tam's face, blinding him with lager.

'Ye auld bastard,' roared Tam, wiping his eyes with the back of his hands, then unzipping the top of his anorak to wipe his neck as he wriggled about to ease his discomfort. 'That lager's fuckin' frozen,' he added in an anguished tone. 'As if I'm no' wet enough.'

Eventually he calmed down and glared at Davey as though wondering how best to deal with him. At that point Davey said, 'Ye can have the golf ba's then.'

He took the golf balls out from his pocket and flung them on the mud floor one by one, but only five of them. Tam looked down at the golf balls like a dog distracted by a bone. Then he glared back at Davey, clenching his fists.

'Listen, you,' he began to say when a voice from the doorway spoke.

'I say, you fellows, have either of you seen a red golf ball? I hit it in this direction and I'm damned if I can see it anywhere.'

The speaker wore a short yellow oilskin with its hood tied tightly under his chin. What could be seen of his face was fat and ruddy-cheeked. He could have been any age between thirty and forty, and he was holding a golf-club. Tam turned and snarled, 'Naw, we huvnae,' the rage still plain on his face. The golfer's eyes narrowed when he saw the golf balls lying on the mud.

'You've been stealing our golf balls, I see.'

'We never stole them,' said Tam. 'We found them and they're oors.'

The golfer laughed unpleasantly. 'You can tell that to the manager for I'm going to report you as soon as I get back to the club.'

'Report away,' said Tam with an equally unpleasant laugh.

'In the mean time,' said the golfer, 'you can give me up those golf balls and I might let you away with it this time. That is,' he wagged an admonishing finger at Tam, 'if I don't ever see either of you up here again.'

He then addressed Davey, who had never moved off the bench, sitting with his empty can of lager in his hand and his legs crossed like a disinterested onlooker.

'As for you, you're always up here pinching our golf balls. You definitely should be reported.'

He was about to say a lot more, when Tam tapped him on the shoulder with a look of disbelief on his face and said, 'Dae you mean to say ye want me tae bend doon and pick up these ba's and personally haund them ower tae you?'

'Exactly.'

'That'll be right,' said Tam as he began to kick them one by one under the bench. 'If you want them get them yersel'.'

'Right,' said the golfer, his cheeks turning purple. 'I will and you'll definitely be reported.'

As he bent down to retrieve them Tam gave him a shove. The golfer landed flat on the mud, his nose barely missing the bench. Tam let out a guffaw of laughter.

'There wis nae need for that,' said Davey helping the golfer to his feet and making feeble attempts to wipe the mud off his chin. The golfer backed off outside the doorway shaking his fist.

'Just wait' he shouted, 'I'll be back with my mates. You've both had it, I can tell you.' His voice became fainter as he vanished round the side of the hut.

'I soon got rid o' him,' said Tam to Davey as if nothing amiss had happened between them. Then he froze and pointed outwards. 'Christ, he's left his golf-club.' He picked it up and went outside to hit great chunks of moss into the air, calling to Davey, 'This is a' right. I think I'll have a go roon the park wi' this club.'

Davey placed his empty can under the bench and came out into the open.

'We'd best get crackin' afore these golfers come back.'

They were a good bit down the path when Tam said, 'Christ the golf ba's. I forgot them,' and ran back towards the hut.

Davey kept walking, hoping the golfers would meet up with Tam and beat him to a pulp. It didn't happen. Tam came back five minutes later, his pockets bulging.

'Fancy forgetting them,' he said, laughing.

Davey looked behind. When he saw there was no one following, he said to Tam, 'You walk on. I cannae keep up wi' ye.'

'I'll walk slow,' said Tam. 'I came oot wi' ye. I might as well go back wi' ye.' Then after a pause he reached into his pocket, adding, 'You can take four

21

ba's back and that'll be four each. That's fair enough, isn't it?'

'Very fair,' said Davey, just wanting to get rid of Tam at all costs.

Tam went on, 'Dae ye know whit I've been thinkin'?'

'Naw – whit?'

'I've been thinkin' I'll gie ma golf ba's and the club to the young yins that hit ba's roon the park. It's a bloody shame they cannae afford tae play on a real course. Dae ye no' think it would be a nice gesture?'

'Very nice indeed,' said Davey after picking up a red golf ball halfway down the path. Tam didn't notice, being bemused with his thoughts.

They reached the fence, climbed over it and were crossing the fields when Tam said, 'Dae ye know, I enjoyed masel' the day. It's a great wee hobby collectin' golf ba's. But the next time we go we should try that private course up at Lynmoor. We can always get the bus up. It's no that dear – '

He broke off as Davey began to run – not very fast though because of his wellingtons for one thing and his age for another. Tam caught up with him easily. He said, 'Whit's wrang wi' you. Are you in a huff or somethin'?'

THE WAREHOUSE

T he middle-aged couple sat with their backs against the wall. Some drunks against the opposite wall shouted on them to come over.

'Ignore them. They'll only be wanting some of our drink. I thought that fellow with the mouth-organ would have come back this evening. Still, it's early yet.'

'What fellow?' asked the man.

'The one who was here last Friday. Remember he played some good, old-fashioned tunes. There was one I liked in particular. It was kind of Mexican – '

'I don't remember.'

'At the time, you said you knew it. You were even singing the words – '

'I don't remember,' said the man emphatically. 'What's more important is this bottle's nearly empty. We'll have to get another.'

The woman pursed her lips. 'There's plenty left in that bottle. Don't be so desperate – ' She broke off when she saw the warehouse door slide open and a young woman stand within the gap.

'Come in and close the door. There's a draught!' she shouted.

The young woman closed the door behind her then called out that she couldn't see a thing.

'You will when you get used to it. How do you think we manage?'

The young woman made her way across the floor, sat beside them and explained that she'd only looked in because she'd heard voices. The older woman said, 'That's all right. It's a free country. So what's your name?'

'Jessica.'

'That's a pretty name.'

The woman thought that seen close up this Jessica looked much more mature than from a distance, with her dyed-blonde hair and heavily pencilled eyebrows.

'My name's Mavis and this is my friend Albert,' she said, gesturing towards the man. He had glanced briefly at the young woman when she came in but now sat staring at the floor. Mavis offered Jessica the bottle.

'Thanks all the same but I'd rather have a temazepam or a fag if you've got one to spare.'

'We've no temazepam but it so happens I've got fags,' said Mavis, bringing a packet of Embassy Regal from her coat pocket. She offered it to Jessica then Albert before taking one herself. After the initial puff she began to cough.

'These fags will be the death of me.'

'Don't get my hopes built up,' said Albert suddenly, winking at Jessica. She gave him a polite smile back. Mavis asked him why he looked so pleased all of a sudden when he hadn't had a civil word to say all day.

'Me pleased?' he said, surprised. 'What makes you think I'm pleased?'

'Never mind,' she said, becoming downcast for no reason she could think of, then suddenly furious because Jessica had turned to the drunks on the opposite side of the warehouse and was actually smiling at them.

'Here, don't you be giving them alckies the eye or they'll be over like a shot and we definitely don't want that. At least I don't.'

'Are you talking to me?' said Jessica, her eyes glittering narrowly.

'Who else?'

Jessica made to rise. 'I'm not stopping to be insulted by the likes of you.'

'Don't then.'

By this time Mavis had taken a strong dislike to this young woman, who she thought looked more and more like a tart with every minute that passed. She turned to Albert.

'You can see she's only out to cause trouble.'

'Leave her alone and mind your own bloody business,' he said.

Rage boiled up inside her. She lifted the bottle and smashed it against the wall splashing it with wine. Some dribbled to the floor. There was a silence in which the three of them stared at the small, dark-red puddle.

Finally Albert said, 'There must have been at least a good third left in that bottle.' He stood up and Mavis thought he was going to strike her. Instead he went over to Jessica and asked if she would like to come outside.

'If you want,' she said jumping up and taking his arm.

Open-mouthed, in a state of shock, Mavis watched them leave. By the time she'd pulled herself together and hurried out after them they had vanished. She hung about for a good while in the hope Albert would regret what he'd done and come back. Perhaps the whole thing had been his idea of a joke or even a punishment. Albert could be very devious. No one knew better than she how devious, but when time passed without any sign of him, she was forced to move away, unsure of everything.

Fifteen minutes later she entered the licensed grocer to buy another bottle. It was all she could think to do although she hadn't intended drinking again so soon.

'Your friend, he is not with you this evening?' asked Abdul, who took a personal interest in the affairs of his customers.

Mavis explained that it appeared he'd left her for another woman.

'But that is terrible. What has come over him?'

She then went on to say that it must be because of his age for according to what she'd heard, lots of men leave their wives or partners for younger women when they reach a certain age: the male menopause, it's called, and as the woman he'd gone off with appeared young enough to be his daughter, that's all she could put it down to.

'Perhaps he will regret it later on,' said Abdul, shaking his head in dismay, then wrapping up the bottle in brown paper and giving it an extra twist at the top. Mavis always felt like telling him not to bother with the paper as it only got thrown away but she never did in case she hurt his feelings.

She went out the door, promising to let him know of any further developments. Outside she threw away the paper, unscrewed the top of the bottle and took a long gulp of the wine. It immediately put new heart into her. She began to see the affair from a different angle. If Albert never came back she would be better off without him in many ways. She wouldn't have to put up with his foul moods when he had drunk too much, nor would she have to keep him going in it when she'd hardly enough for herself. Nor would she be obliged to have sex when she didn't feel like it. She hadn't felt like it for years, come to think of it. There were hundreds of things she wouldn't feel obliged to do in order to shut his mouth. Why, life without Albert might not be so bad after all. Instead of spending half her next giro on him, she would get something decent to wear from the Oxfam shop, then have her hair done – nothing fancy, a cut and blow dry would do her fine. Then after that (her heart pounded at the idea) she would go to the local housing department and ask for her name to be put down on the list for a council flat. It was time she got in off the streets and started having a decent life for a change.

As she walked along the pavement, her head quite dizzy with thinking about the great possibilities that lay ahead, she bumped into a woman who told her to watch where she was going then tried to push her off the pavement. Mavis's mood quickly changed.

'Who do you think you're shoving?'

'Scum,' said the woman over her shoulder, which depressed Mavis. She recognized the truth of the statement but if Albert had been with her the situation would never have arisen. Coming to a row of tenements, she paused outside an entrance wondering whether to have a drink inside rather than risk taking it in the open, when a young man came from the building and told her to beat it.

'I was only looking for an address,' she said as he brushed past. He exuded an air of violence which left her dithering and too frightened to move. Her previous confidence vanished. The truth of the matter, she told herself sadly, was that on her own she could scarcely walk two steps without somebody picking on her. What a fool she'd been! She'd just have to throw her pride to the wind and go and find Albert then persuade him to come back to her. She'd buy him all the drink he needed and he could bring Jessica with him if that's what he wanted. Anything was better than being on her own. He couldn't be far away. She'd try the old warehouse first. The chances were he might be there already, waiting for her to bring along the bottle.

'Albert,' she called, entering the warehouse and leaving the door open so that she could see her way. There was no answer but it was still early, perhaps not eight o'clock yet. She reached the spot where they usually sat, and took a small sip of wine, assuring herself she would make it last until Albert arrived. Otherwise he wouldn't be pleased. To pass the time she smoked three cigarettes. After finishing the third she'd become so jumpy that without thinking she put the bottle to her mouth and took a long swig and became so fuddled that she forgot all about Albert and Jessica. The only thing in her mind now was the Mexican tune the man with the mouth-organ had played the previous Friday. The words that had eluded her before came into her head quite easily.

The mission bells told me, that I mustn't stay,
South of the border, down Mexico way.

In her cracked voice she sang the whole verse and continued singing it over and over again. She stopped once when she thought she heard footsteps outside.

'Is that you, Albert?' she called, but when there was no reply she simply carried on singing, enjoying the sound of her voice and only breaking off now and again to put the bottle to her mouth. She finally stopped when it grew so dark that she couldn't see a thing. This gave her a creepy feeling. She picked up the bottle and discovered it was empty. Immediately she felt horrifyingly sober. The only thing to do was to try and sleep if she could.

'Dear God,' she prayed as she sometimes did when desperate enough, 'just let me sleep through this night and I'll not touch another drop. Or at least,' she amended, not wanting to commit herself entirely, 'I'll cut it down a bit.'

After that she lit a cigarette, inhaled deeply, and as if in answer to her prayer her eyelids began to droop. She settled back against the wall and fell asleep, the cigarette dangling from her lips. It dropped onto her coat. The smouldering tip touched particles of fluff which eventually burst into flames.

WHEN SHANKLAND COMES

I t was a raw March morning when Ivy came into the village hotel where she was employed as a cleaner. Sometimes she served in the public bar, but at present she wasn't needed there, for trade was always poor after the New Year. In summer, though, the hotel did well. It stood on the main road and was a good stopping point for tourists on their way to the mountains and lochs beyond. The village itself could be described as sleepy. Some folks said it was merely dull. On the side of the road near the hotel was a long stretch of mansions; on the other, a grocery store and a small scheme of neat, one-storey council houses. Behind the scheme stood a church dated 1894 and refaced with pink modern brick. There was no school in the village. The kids, big and small, travelled by bus to the small town of Blairmaddie five miles away.

There were only two customers in the public bar: Geordie Forsyth, the builder, and Sam Ferguson, who was elderly and toothless. Geordie Forsyth watched Ivy wipe the bar counter. She was tall and angular-faced with an abundance of dark curling hair and a slim figure under a green nylon overall. Though almost forty, older men – including Geordie Forsyth – found her attractive.

'Ye look fair scunnered,' Geordie said.

'That's no crime,' said Ivy, tossing her head. Her mind was on Dennett, her seventeen-year-old son. He had refused to get out of bed when she called him up for work and he'd only started the job on the farm two days before. Admittedly, it was on the side and the wage was poor, but added to his social security money, she thought he would be doing fine. When she called him a lazy bastard, he'd said, well, it wasn't his fault if he was a bastard, was it? The remark had rankled. It still rankled.

'Gie us a smile,' said Geordie, when she lifted his glass to wipe under it. 'Ye're braw when ye smile.'

'I'm no' in the mood for smilin' said Ivy; nevertheless, her mouth softened. She liked Geordie well enough. He wasn't bad looking in a coarse way and he had a steady job, which said a lot in his favour, but she didn't trust him. He was a hard drinker. Everybody knew that was why his wife had left him. Anyway, she'd never had any time for men since Dennett was born.

'Whit she needs is a man,' said old Sam, wheezing with laughter.

'That I don't need,' said Ivy, rubbing away furiously. 'Besides there's no men in this place, at least no' what I'd call one.'

'Come roon the back and I'll soon show ye,' said Geordie.

Sam laughed again. Ivy tutted and said to Geordie, 'You

should be at your buildin' instead of standin' here drinking. I don't know how you get away wi' it.'

'Because I'm ma ain boss,' said Geordie complacently, just as Jim Carr, the barman, came in.

'Hurry up wi' that counter so as I can get servin',' he told Ivy. Geordie put down his empty tumbler on the counter and walked out. Old Sam faded into the background, holding a glass which still contained an inch of beer.

'Who is there to serve?' snapped Ivy, and headed for the kitchen. It was almost ten o'clock and time for her cup of tea. Going down the hallway she met Walter Sproul, the manager. Although he barely glanced at her, she noted the bags under his eyes. Likely been on the bottle last night, she thought, and fighting with his wife. They could be heard first thing in the morning, either brawling at each other or thumping on their bed in a frenzy of lovemaking. Ivy despised Sproul and also that wife of his. She did absolutely nothing in the hotel except come down the stairs in the afternoon, her hair all frizzed up and her make-up thick, and drive off somewhere in her blue Mercedes. Of course when Shankland came it was a different story. Then you'd see her hovering behind Sproul as he spoke to Shankland with a smarmy smile on his face. Albert Shankland had been manager when Ivy first started work twenty years ago. She had been taken on part time as a waitress, then full time when he'd asked her to clean. The hotel had done well in those days. It had always been a pleasure to work for Shankland. Eventually he had bought the hotel and then another one farther south. Soon after, he'd moved south himself, appointing a new manager in his place. It had been a bitter blow, but that was a long time ago. Many managers had come and gone before Sproul took over. Sproul, though, was the worst. She wished Shankland would pay the hotel one of his flying visits to study the books and give a pep talk to the staff. He always took her aside and spoke to her in a warm and friendly way. Once he even enquired about Dennett. 'He's fine,' she'd answered, not knowing what else to say.

In the big kitchen, Babs, the cook, was pouring out two cups of tea. Ivy began to spread butter thickly on a roll.

'That Sproul gets on ma goat,' Babs said.

'What's he done this time?' said Ivy.

'He says we'll have tae put less meat in the sandwiches.' Staring hard at Ivy's roll, she added, 'He'll go mad if he sees that.'

'I'm no' takin' any meat,' Ivy pointed out.

'I've got tae account for the butter as well,' said Babs, her voice aggrieved.

Ivy shrugged then sat up on a high stool with her back facing the table and her legs crossed. Babs frowned at the sight of Ivy's slim legs. Her own were short and fat. In fact she was fat all over, with a stomach that bulged out under her white overall. Her broad face was red from the heat of the kitchen.

'By the way,' she said, are you goin' tae the dance in the church hall on Saturday?'

Ivy wrinkled her nose slightly. 'I don't know. They're gettin' awful stale nowadays.'

'Ye always get a laugh at somethin', and the punch is free.'

'I'm no' that desperate for a drink,' said Ivy.

'There's nothin' much else happenin' in this dump,' said Babs bitterly.

'If I go, it means that Dennett's in the house by himsel' until dead late.'

'Surely Dennett's auld enough to stay in by hissel'?'

'I'll have to think about it,' said Ivy, picturing Dennett bringing his pals in and drinking cans of lager.

Ivy was washing her cup when Jim burst into the kitchen and asked her to take the bar while he had some tea, since Betty, the lounge bar waitress, hadn't come in yet.

'I don't know how she's kept on,' said Ivy. 'She's always late.'

'And she's that bloody cheeky wi' it tae,' said Babs.

'Yous two are just jealous because she's sexy lookin',' Jim said.

Ivy and Babs laughed simultaneously. 'She's as sexy lookin' as a coo lookin' ower a dyke,' said Ivy.

There was nobody in the bar except old Sam, still holding his tumbler with its inch of beer.

'Finish that pint and get anither one,' said Ivy. 'This is no' a bus shelter you're staunin' in.'

'I cannae afford anither one,' said Sam. 'I've only got ma pension tae keep me.'

'Aye, I know,' said Ivy sighing. She was about to give him a free half-pint when Betty came in, her blonde hair spiked at the top and long and flat at the back.

'I slept in,' she explained, as old Sam gave her a startled look. He finished his beer and walked stiffly away.

'I'm sure that hair-do must have taken a good hour to fix,' said Ivy.

'No' really,' said Betty. 'It's quite easy when ye know how.'

Sensing that Betty was about to launch into a long explanation about why she'd slept in, Ivy said quickly, 'Now that you're in, I'm away to clean the toilets.'

The day passed slowly for Ivy. Business was still poor in the afternoon, apart from a few young lads from the community programme who came in to order coffee. She looked at them enviously as they came through the hotel door wearing their donkey jackets. She wished Dennett could have been one of them. Of course he was too young for the community programme which mainly consisted of doing old folks' gardens. In bad weather they hung around the hotel entrance, laughing loud and inanely, but at least they were obliged to get up in the morning. Dennett had still been in bed when she went home at lunch-time.

Sproul's wife left as usual in her Mercedes and Sproul went prowling about the hotel like a pregnant cat, his face sullen and brooding as if looking for someone to lash out at. Ivy affected to look busy by polishing the hallway twice before she went through to the kitchen to scrub the big table. Babs had gone off duty at four o'clock and the room was empty. Ivy stared up through the kitchen window at the tormented-looking sky, thinking that it wouldn't be long till summer when the place would be packed out.

On her way home she stopped at the grocery which sold everything from a packet of pins to a jar of boiled mussels. The freezer near the door was filled with all sorts of frozen packets and half the counter was taken up with rolls, pies and doughnuts, all in separate cardboard boxes. Scarcely four people could stand inside the shop comfortably.

'My, it's a right cauld day,' said Mrs Braithwaite, the owner, from behind the counter. She was a small, stout, elderly woman who always wore a hairnet over her blue perm.

'I'm fair roastin',' said Ivy, and went on to ask for two pies and a tin of beans.

'It'll be a' that hard work ye dae in the hotel,' said Mrs Braithwaite. She put two pies in a poke, then without turning round, lifted a tin of beans from the shelf behind her. The shop was so cramped that she scarcely needed to move an inch to put her hand on any item, except those in the freezer to which folk helped themselves. 'I've heard the manager's no' very easy tae work for,' she added.

'He's no' bad,' said Ivy, reluctant to say anything that could get to Sproul's ears.

'They tell me the wages are no' very good,' said Mrs Braithwaite, when Ivy handed over a pound note for the purchases.

'They're a lot better than what ye get off the social,' said Ivy promptly.

'That's true,' said Mrs Braithwaite, opening the till, 'though I've heard there's plenty on the social and workin' forbye.' She looked directly at Ivy. 'I don't think that's fair, dae you?'

'I don't suppose it is,' said Ivy, wondering if the storekeeper knew that Dennett had worked two days on the farm. She asked for ten king-size Regal before Mrs Braithwaite could pursue the subject any further and headed for the door.

Outside the wind blew cold but invigorating in her face. Old autumn leaves stirred at the side of the pavement and in the distance she saw the peaks of the mountains covered in snow. She walked up the neat path of her council house noting the snowdrops under her window and reflecting that the village would be a nice enough place to stay in if it wasn't for some of the folk.

When she came into the living-room Dennett was sitting in the armchair facing the television with the gas fire turned up full.

'So, you've managed to get up then,' she said, turning the fire low. He stretched his legs and kept his sharp profile fixed ahead. She noticed with distaste that his hair was uncombed. It lay on his shoulders, light brown and straggly. 'You might have washed yersel' at least,' she muttered, as she went through to the kitchenette to put on the kettle. A minute later she was startled to see him towering above her, looking anxious.

'Did ye get my fags?' he asked.

'They're in my bag,' she said, exasperated. 'Do ye no' think it's terrible I should have to buy you fags and you'll no' even make an attempt to earn money to buy them yersel'?'

'I wisnae feelin' well this mornin',' he said, ripping the Cellophane from the packet. 'I'll go tae work the morra.'

'Well, ye'd better,' she said, a bit mollified by this statement. 'But mind,' she added, 'don't go near the store on your way to the farm. If auld Braithwaite thinks you're workin' she could report ye. She's that type.'

'Aye,' he said, then: 'Are ye makin' chips?'

'No,' she shouted, thinking that Dennett never seemed to give a damn about anything that really mattered.

★   ★   ★

'Did ye hear that Shankland's comin'?' Babs said to Ivy when she came into the hotel kitchen next morning.

'When?' said Ivy, trying not to look excited.

'Either Friday or Saturday,' said Babs. She added morosely, 'I hate when he comes.'

'He's OK – a lot better than Sproul,' said Ivy. 'If Shankland has anythin' to say he tells ye fair and square, no' like Sproul wi' his snidy remarks for no good reason. Shankland doesnae bother me.'

'It's a' right for you,' said Babs. 'You're mair familiar wi' him than me.'

'Whit dae ye mean "familiar"?' said Ivy, her voice sharp.

'I only mean that you've known him longer than any of us, that's a',' said Babs, her eyes wide and innocent. She poured out the tea while Ivy buttered her roll heavily. 'Anyway,' she went on, 'business is that bad I wouldnae be surprised if he's up tae close the hotel. It's happenin' a' ower the place. I heard the hotel outside Blairmaddie's tae close and it only opened three years ago.'

Ivy made no comment on this, inwardly seething at the use of the word 'familiar'. It looked as though Babs was jealous of her long acquaintanceship with Shankland. She'd have to be careful of what she said to her in future. When she was washing her cup at the sink Babs said, 'Are ye still no' goin' tae the dance?'

'Definitely no',' snapped Ivy, marching off to dust and hoover the lounge, although she didn't think it would need much cleaning since it hadn't been opened since Monday.

Thursday was cold, but bright. The hotel was surprisingly

busy with families tempted out for the day by the early spring sun, and some of the wealthy retired locals from the big houses. The lounge was opened and there were six men standing in the public bar, including Geordie Forsyth who came in every day anyway. Ivy was asked to serve in the bar while Betty did the lounge. All this and the fact that Dennett had got out of his bed and gone to his job at the farm put Ivy in a good mood. Jim hummed tunes under his breath as he pulled the pints and Sproul walked between the lounge and the bar with his face less haunted looking than usual. Only Babs in the kitchen was grumbling when Ivy dashed in for a quick cup of tea; she hadn't time for a roll.

'If it's goin' tae be as busy as this,' she said, 'I'll need extra help.'

'I thought you said the hotel might be closin' down,' Ivy laughed.

'If it's no' one way it's another,' Babs shouted as Ivy dashed off. 'Don't forget one swallow doesnae make a summer.'

Ivy didn't go home for lunch as she had a lot of cleaning to do. She took a snack in the kitchen then carried on with the washing, the hoovering and dusting, the polishing. It was hard going, she thought, but worth it with the place so busy. From now on maybe business would pick up and everyone would be in a better mood. She got home at half-past five after stopping at the store to buy milk, bread and cheese. Her face fell. Dennett sat in the chair facing the television with the gas fire turned up full.

'I thought ye didnae stop until six,' she said, blinking nervously.

'I've been sacked,' he said.

'Sacked?' she said, throwing her message bag on the couch and sinking down beside it.

'Aye, sacked,' he said defiantly. 'It wis because I never came in yesterday. I've been in here since nine in the mornin'.'

'I knew this would happen,' she said bitterly.

Dennett's voice was equally bitter. 'I'm glad I wis sacked. You don't know whit it's like tae muck out dung all day, and then havin' tae eat your piece wi' yer haunds all smelly, and no' even a drap o' tea to wash it down. Anyway it wisnae a real job, I'd only have got paid in washers.'

'Did you get yer two days' money then?'

'Naw, he said I wis tae come back on Saturday.'

'And I bet like hell you bloody well won't,' said Ivy, her temper rising. 'And here's me workin' my pan in to keep you in meals and fags and put a good face on everythin' and tryin' to keep decent and there you are tellin' me you're above muckin' out byres . . . Well, I don't particularly like bein' a cleaner and gettin' paid in washers either, but I have to do it to keep a roof above our heids.'

Dennett sneered, 'That's up tae you.'

Enraged, Ivy jumped up from the couch and slapped him on the cheek. Dennett confronted her with eyes blazing. For a second she thought he was going to slap her back, but he only stared at her madly for a moment before he rushed out of the room. She heard his bedroom door slam hard, then silence. She sat down on the couch again, drained, vowing to herself that she would tell Dennett to get out. He was old enough to take care of himself, after all; why should she put up with his laziness and cheek? He could get himself a room or a bed-and-breakfast somewhere in Blairmaddie, and come to think of it, Blairmaddie would suit him better, being full of licensed grocers and pubs.

Knowing him, he'd likely just drift around spending his social money on booze or even dope: she'd heard there were junkies galore there. At least, she thought angrily, if he's out of the way he can't give me a showing-up in the village. She sat for a while thinking of what could happen to Dennett in Blairmaddie or some other bigger place beyond. But she could never do it, of course. He was too feckless. It was quite beyond her to put him out at seventeen. Besides, he wouldn't go easily, and after all he might get a job with the community programme next September when he was eighteen. Sighing, she stood up and went through to the kitchenette to make some tea and toasted cheese. It was all she felt fit to cook. Ten minutes later she shouted from the living-room, 'Dennett, come and get your supper.' When he came through he peered at the plate on the worktop, saying in a perplexed manner, 'Toasted cheese? How did ye no' make chips for a change?'

On Friday it snowed and again there was hardly anybody in the bar except Geordie Forsyth, who was at one of the tables in the small room, deep in discussion with two of the brickies he employed. He hardly glanced at Ivy when she came in to clean, which annoyed her in a way, especially when she had taken extra pains with her hair, brushing it hard so that it fell smoothly round her face, as well as putting on a touch of eye-shadow and lipstick. Although all this was for Shankland's benefit, she'd expected a compliment or two from Geordie. Betty came in right on time for once, and Ivy didn't doubt that it was because she too expected Shankland at any minute. Jim stood behind Betty, polishing the glasses intently.

The morning passed and Shankland did not show up, nor was there any sign of Sproul in the hotel. This seemed strange to Ivy but she didn't remark on it, not even to Babs. In fact, they had scarcely a word to say to each other during the tea break. It was as if they had mutually decided to fall out.

Ivy came back home at lunch feeling thoroughly disgruntled. She was taken aback to see Dennett up and fully clothed, eating toast and scrambled egg. Then she remembered that this was his giro day.

'There's some egg left in the pot,' he said obligingly.

'Thanks,' she said curtly, thinking he'd have done better to make a slice of toast to go with it. Before she left she reminded him to leave his money on the sideboard after he had cashed the giro at Braithwaite's store.

'I always dae,' he answered with a touch of indignation.

In the afternoon when she took the Hoover into the lounge, she was surprised to see Sproul's wife standing behind the small lounge bar.

'Don't bother hoovering,' she told Ivy. 'The carpet's clean enough. Just separate the tables. They're far too close together.'

'I always hoover the carpet whether it's clean or no',' Ivy said hotly. 'That's how it's in such good condition.'

'Nonsense,' said Sproul's wife. 'Just do as I say.'

'Wait a minute,' said Ivy, her eyes blazing. 'Since when have you taken charge?'

Sproul's wife said tartly, 'As from today, I'm in charge of the lounge.' As Ivy stared at her in disbelief, Sproul's wife, her lips cyclamen pink and smiling, added, 'If you don't believe me, ask my husband when he comes in.'

'I'll no' bother seein' your husband,' Ivy retorted, 'I'll wait tae Shankland comes in. It seems to me he's the main one to see.'

'Do you think so?' said Sproul's wife, assuming an astonished expression. 'I'd hardly credit that, when my husband is paid to manage the hotel. However, if you want to see Mr Shankland you'll have to wait until tomorrow. He's down at Blairmaddie at the moment discussing business with my husband in the Riverbank Hotel. He thought it better to stay there for the night on account of the roads being so bad up here with the snow.'

Ivy gave Sproul's wife one black look, then turned on her heels, trailing the Hoover behind her.

'What about separating the tables,' Sproul's wife called, but Ivy was off into the toilet to try and calm herself down.

On a Friday at teatime the store was always busy, mainly with women rushing in at the last minute after collecting their husbands' wages. Although there was less rushing in nowadays than there used to be, it was still busy enough to make Ivy fume with impatience as she waited at the end of the queue. She wanted to get home quickly to make sure that her share of Dennett's giro was lying on the sideboard, but beside that, she had been thrown into confusion by her encounter with Sproul's wife. It seemed as she waited that Mrs Braithwaite was chatting longer than ever with the customers. When finally her turn came she asked in a clipped voice for bread, potatoes and half a pound of sausages. This didn't prevent the storekeeper informing her that Dennett had just been in to cash his giro. As Ivy nodded and opened her purse, Mrs Braithwaite added, 'It's a pity he cannae get work, a big strong fella like that.'

Ivy was stung into saying, 'There's no work to be had, is there?'

'I don't know,' said Mrs Braithwaite deliberately. 'There's some that widnae take a job if it was under their very nose.'

Ivy grabbed her change from Mrs Braithwaite's fat fingers and marched out past the queue that had formed behind her.

When she went in through the front door she heard Dennett running the tap in the bathroom. He usually celebrated his giro day with a bath and a hair wash before going out with his pals for a night in Blairmaddie. She put the kettle on then checked to see if her money was on the sideboard. It was – the whole twenty-five pounds of it. His dinner was on the plate when he came into the kitchen, rubbing his hair with a towel, his face pink and shiny.

'Good', he said. 'Chips.'

'I'm glad somethin' pleases you,' she said drily, following him into the living-room. Dennett stuffed chips into his mouth, gazing dreamily at the television. Ivy picked at her meal half-heartedly. Before she lifted the dishes to wash them, she told Dennett to mind and go up to the farm on Saturday and get the money owed to him.

'Aye – so I wull,' he said reluctantly, frowning as if he had no intention of going at all. Then he stood up and went into his bedroom. Within seconds the insistent beat of some pop group pounded on her ear-drums. She debated whether to go through and tell him to turn the sound down. Instead, she took a pair of ear-plugs from a drawer in the kitchen cabinet and sat down on the couch, staring blankly at a television she couldn't hear. An hour later he peeped into the living-room to tell her that he was away. She took the ear-plugs out and told him not to be late.

'Aye, so I wull,' he said. She knew she was wasting her breath.

On Saturday, rain turned the snow on the pavements to slush. Ivy came into the public bar wearing a blue woollen dress minus her nylon apron. She had decided to look good for Shankland, but when Jim turned to her and said, 'For a second I thought you wir Sproul's wife,' she began to wonder if the dress was a mistake.

'I should hope no',' she muttered, dying to ask him if Shankland had come in last night. Pride kept her silent. She asked if Sproul was around.

'No' yit,' he answered, pulling a face as if something was happening that only he knew about. When she began to wipe the shelves he said in a low voice, 'Sproul's wife is takin' over the lounge.'

'So I heard,' said Ivy. 'Well, maybe it's time she did something for her keep.'

'Looks as if there's gaun to be a lot mair changes,' said Jim darkly.

Curtly, Ivy replied, 'It's all one tae me, I'm only the cleaner, thank God.'

Jim turned away to serve one of the men who had come

forward from a youngish crowd sitting at a table. Every Saturday morning they came in, deafening the place with their loud aggressive talk. Ivy was glad to get out of the bar whenever they arrived.

'Would ye like to gie us a hand?' Jim asked her when another two came forward to the counter.

'I've got a lot to do,' said Ivy, hurrying away: Betty would be in any minute and she'd be overjoyed to serve that boisterous lot.

'That's a nice dress ye've on,' Babs said to her in the kitchen, evidently prepared to be friendly.

'Actually, it's quite an old one,' said Ivy.

'It doesnae look it,' said Babs. 'How have ye no' got yer apron on? It'll get a' dirty.'

'I forgot to bring it. Anyway, it doesnae matter if it gets dirty,' said Ivy impatiently.

'Here, d'ye know that Sproul's wife's in the lounge?' said Babs, handing Ivy a cup of tea and a roll which she explained was already buttered.

'Thanks,' said Ivy, suspecting the roll would be buttered thin. 'She telt me herself yesterday.'

'Did she?' said Babs, her eyes wide. 'You must be well in. Naebody tells me anythin' except when it's history.'

'I wouldn't worry about it,' said Ivy. 'There's always bound to be changes at some time.'

'Aye, but changes are never for the best nowadays,' said Babs.

'Let's look on the bright side for once,' said Ivy, feeling anything but bright. She suddenly had a premonition: either Shankland wasn't going to come in at all, or maybe he had been in last night and gone away again. So if Sproul's wife

51

was going to take over the lounge where did that leave her? If Betty had only the public bar to do, it meant that they wouldn't need her to serve at all and there definitely wasn't enough cleaning to justify her hours from nine to five. And if they cut her hours, she might as well be on the dole. She'd have to talk to Sproul about it immediately.

Suddenly Babs said, 'Are you still no' goin' tae the dance?'

'I've already told you I'm no',' said Ivy sharply.

'Then I don't think I'll go either,' said Babs. 'I hate goin' in the door masel'.'

'Don't then,' said Ivy. She felt like screaming.

Later, when she was coming out of the toilet, Betty told her in a casual way that she'd heard Shankland was coming in the afternoon. Ivy brightened up at that. She decided that there was no need to see Sproul. Shankland would allay her fears. So what if Sproul's wife was managing the lounge? She could come to terms with that as long as they didn't cut her hours.

When she got home at lunch-time she looked in at Dennett's room to see if he was all right. Heaven knows what time he'd come home last night, and in what condition. When she'd left this morning she had been so preoccupied by the affairs of the hotel that she'd forgotten all about him. She found him lying on his back, snoring his head off, his long legs sticking out from under the blankets. 'Dennett,' she called, but he continued to snore. When she called again, 'Do ye want something to eat?' he grunted, 'Naw,' and turned on his side. She studied him for a while, almost envying his complete disregard for anyone but himself. He had no talent, no ambition and no pride, yet he looked so happy lying there with that slight smile on his lips.

The afternoon wore on and still there was no sign of Shankland. Sproul passed her once or twice as she was polishing the woodwork in the corridor, and ducked his head in an embarrassed way which made her wonder. But when Jim handed over her pay-packet at half-past four, she found out why. Inside was two weeks' money and a letter saying that due to increased overheads and poor trade, the management regretted that they no longer required her services. However, as soon as trade picked up they would send for her again.

Ivy scanned the letter twice to make sure she had read correctly. Then chalk-faced, she went off in search of Sproul. She found him behind the lounge bar, standing close to his wife. They were studying a ledger and they looked conspiratorial. Ivy thrust the letter under Sproul's nose and said, 'You cannae do this to me.'

Sproul and his wife looked up at her with pained expressions. Sproul said, 'I'm very sorry about this, but . . .'

'Never mind bein' sorry,' Ivy interrupted. 'I'm goin' to see Shankland. When will he be in?'

Sproul's wife shoved her face forward. 'He won't be in,' she said spitefully. 'He's already spoken to us about everything. Isn't that right, Walter?'

'Yes,' Sproul said heavily.

Ivy's head swam. She said faintly, 'He cannae know about this. Shankland would never sack me.'

'It was his instructions,' said Sproul.

'You're lyin',' said Ivy. 'Give me his address and I'll get in touch wi' him masel'.'

Sproul and his wife exchanged weary glances.

'Look Ivy,' said Sproul, 'if you want to see him, try the church hall round about ten o'clock. He and his wife have been invited to the dance as special guests, but I can assure you that letter was written on his instructions.'

'I still don't believe you,' said Ivy, turning away to hide the tears in her eyes. A minute later she put on her coat and walked out of the hotel without saying a word to anyone.

Prompt at ten, Ivy was inside the church hall, still wearing her blue woollen dress and fortified by two glasses of port from the bottle which had been in her sideboard since the New Year. She was dismayed to see hardly anyone but the minister and some church elders waiting by the door. On a platform in a corner near the entrance sat the band wearing maroon shirts and dark suits, the same band that played every year, its members middle-aged and bespectacled. The minister's wife and her cronies stood at the far end of the hall beside a table spread with food. Hesitantly, Ivy went over to the table and, for want of anything better to do, helped herself to a sandwich and a glass of punch from the big fruit bowl in the centre.

'How nice to see you, Ivy,' said the minister's wife, smiling horsily.

'Likewise, I'm sure,' said Ivy. She took a gulp of the punch and shuddered.

'Strong, isn't it?' said the minister's wife. 'There's a bottle of brandy in it. I made it myself.'

'It's very good,' said Ivy, forcing a smile. She added brightly, 'There's no' many turned up though.'

'They'll be fortifyin' themselves in the hotel,' said Mrs

54

Braithwaite, who wore pink gingham and for once had no hairnet on.

'Do you mind if I sit down?' said Ivy. She was beginning to feel dizzy from drinking the strong punch on top of the port. She went over to the bench against the wall and sat there sipping from her glass until she calmed down a bit. A crowd of men and women thrust through the door like cattle from a stockade and the band began to play a slow foxtrot. The minister and his wife were the first on the floor, dancing awkwardly, their faces strained. Ivy decided to have just one more glass of punch. It would while away the time until Shankland arrived, although by now her head was so foggy that quite honestly she didn't really care whether he came or not. When she turned round from the table she saw Babs sailing towards her like a gigantic balloon in her wide orange dress.

'I thought you werenae comin',' said Babs indignantly, helping herself to a sausage roll. With crumbs falling from her mouth, she added, 'Is it true ye've got the sack?'

'Is that what you heard?' said Ivy, taking a gulp of punch.

'Well, is it true?' Babs persisted.

'Nothing that's ever said in this place is true.' Ivy pointed to the bowl of punch. 'Try some of that. It's strong stuff. There's a whole bottle of brandy in it.' She heard herself laugh foolishly.

'It seems tae be,' said Babs, staring hard at Ivy. Then she walked off to talk to the minister's wife, leaving Ivy on her own.

Geordie Forsyth came up from behind and asked her for a dance. She was vaguely surprised to see him so smart in a grey pin-striped suit. 'Right,' she said, grateful for the rescue. As they waltzed round the hall she tripped over his feet, feeling quite giddy.

'Steady on,' said Geordie. He pulled her close, his hand pressing her waist. If it hadn't been for the half bottle in Geordie's pocket jamming hard into her hip, she would happily have floated around the hall for the rest of the night. When the dance ended Geordie asked her if she'd like to come outside for a wee nip of whisky.

'I don't know . . .' she began. And then she saw Shankland standing in the doorway. With him was a small, plump, matronly woman in a black lace dress. Shankland was shaking hands with the minister, his heavy-jowled face lit by a smile. He was a big man with a thick waist. He had never been handsome, exactly, but he attracted attention wherever he went.

Without thinking, Ivy rushed forward. 'Mr Shankland,' she said, tugging at his sleeve, 'can I have a word with you? It's very important.'

Shankland turned round, frowning. 'Later, Ivy. Can't you see my wife and I are talking to the minister?' His wife, who as far as Ivy could see hadn't been talking at all, looked her up and down with suspicion.

'I'm sorry,' said Ivy, 'but Sproul's sacked me from the hotel and I've been waitin' for you to come in.' The words came out slurred. She broke off, sick at heart at Shankland's expression.

'Yes, I'm sorry it had to happen,' he said guardedly. 'But you see, it was either that or closing down the hotel altogether. However, if the place does better in the summer we'll send for you again, don't worry on that score.' And with that he turned back to the minister, who had been listening anxiously.

Suddenly Ivy's rage erupted. 'You mean to say,' she said, her voice rising, 'that you were the one who sacked me, after all these years? All these years I've been loyal and kept my mouth shut?'

Shankland scarcely looked at her. 'Go away, Ivy,' he said wearily. 'You're drunk.'

'Yes, do go and sit down, Ivy,' the minister pleaded. 'You're not your usual self. Perhaps it's the punch. I told my wife not to put in so much brandy.'

'What do you mean − "kept your mouth shut"?' asked Shankland's wife, her face puckering.

'Don't listen to her,' Shankland said. 'She's just upset and a bit drunk. That's all there is to it.' He led his wife towards the table, bending over her slightly, while the minister followed close behind.

Ivy stood for a moment, dazed, her mind fuddled by the slow, monotonous rhythm of the band. She noticed Geordie Forsyth dancing with Babs and looking genteel. A taste of bile was in her mouth and her head was in a turmoil. She saw Shankland turn his back on her and offer his wife a sandwich from a plate. Then all at once her mind was made up. She rushed across to the table.

'That's no' all there is to it!' she said in a voice loud and clear. 'What about Dennett, my son and yours, whom I've kept for seventeen years without a penny off ye? I took the blame on myself, aye, they say it's always the woman to blame, don't they? But since you think so little of me I might as well admit in front of everybody here that you're Dennett's father. I think ye owe me something for that.'

'You're crazy!' said Shankland, with a furtive look at his wife. Her face had turned white as a sheet. All around the table a hush had fallen, and people were staring. He grabbed his wife's elbow. 'Let's get out of here,' he whispered.

The small woman stood her ground, trembling. 'Leave me alone,' she said.

Shankland tugged at her urgently. 'Come on.'

And then his wife's arm jerked up and her eyes went blank and she threw the glass of punch straight into Shankland's face.

'Oh dear,' said the minister, his hands fluttering in the air, and someone laughed. There were a few more titters. Then Shankland turned and marched towards the door, his wife following a yard or two behind.

Ivy clutched at the table for support.

'Go ower and sit down,' Mrs Braithwaite said in a surprisingly kind voice. 'I'll see if I can get a cup of tea from somewhere.' She glared at the minister's wife. 'That punch bowl's been a bloody curse!'

'I'm OK,' said Ivy, smiling wanly.

'I'm awful sorry,' said the minister's wife with an apologetic look at Ivy. 'I shouldn't have put so much brandy in.'

'Don't worry yoursel', I quite enjoyed it.'

Ivy walked over to the bench by the wall and sat down. Geordie Forsyth and Babs came off the dance floor, red-faced and dripping with sweat.

'Have you been sittin' here a' night?' Babs sounded concerned.

'No' really,' said Ivy.

'I thought I saw Shankland come in.'

'So he did,' said Ivy. 'He's away now.'

'Did he say anythin'? I mean, about you gettin' the sack?'

'No' as much as I said to him.'

Geordie took the half bottle from his pocket. 'Do any of yous ladies want a wee nip?'

'No' straight frae the bottle,' said Babs, aghast.

'I'll take one,' said Ivy, putting the bottle to her mouth.

'Will ye look at her!' Babs said. 'To think she's aye sae proud and ladylike.'

'No' any more,' said Ivy. The rough whisky trickled down her throat. She was about to tilt the bottle again when a sudden thought stopped her. Dennett. It wasn't as if she only had herself to consider, after all. Likely he'd be in on his own, watching the television, since he never had any money left on a Saturday to go anywhere. Aye, Dennett. Somebody had to set him an example, didn't they, and she'd been doing it for years so she wasn't about to stop now. She handed the bottle back to Geordie and struggled to her feet. 'I think I'll go home now.'

'Away, it's still early,' said Geordie, looking at his watch.

'I must get home,' Ivy said firmly. 'I've left Dennett in himsel' and he's no' to be trusted.'

'There goes an awfy determined woman,' said Geordie, as he and Babs watched her leave.

'The trouble wi' Ivy,' said Babs, 'is that she's aye been too big for her boots, and now she's been sacked she cannae take it.' She sniffed loudly. 'If you ask me, it serves her right.'

A BAD INFLUENCE

'I don't like you going up to Donald's room,' my mother would say if we were visiting Granny's. 'He's a bad influence and I want you to stay away from him.'

The minute I got there I was upstairs like a shot. Uncle Donald, although only four years older than myself, was the leader of a bunch of guys who came along to play cards and smoke hash. Once they gave me a joint to try and I nearly passed out. The next time I took one I was fine. I had the feeling I was being tested for future membership.

Then there was this dame called Marian who sometimes accompanied them. I noticed she always sat right next to Donald. I'm sure he couldn't have fancied her for she wasn't the least bit attractive. Once she kissed me in front of everybody. I think this was to make Donald jealous but all he said was, 'Leave the kid alone. He's too young for you,' and I hated her for that.

Donald was extra good on the guitar. Apart from playing the stuff everybody played he made up tunes of his own.

They were a bit weird, right enough, like something you hear on Radio 2, but we always acted as though we enjoyed it, except Marian who said she preferred country and western. I expect she thought she was being clever but Donald just shrugged as if he didn't care.

'I hope you're not smoking dope up in that room,' said my mother when I was going back along the road one day.

'Of course not. Only the odd fag or two.'

'For if I ever catch you – '

I walked on ahead so that I couldn't hear her. I wasn't worried though. It would be the usual empty threat.

One evening I went up to the room and no one was there. I dashed down into the living-room

'Where is everybody?'

Granny looked up at me pitifully and shook her head. My mother said she didn't know about everybody but she'd just been told that Donald had run off because he owed the drug-dealer. My heart sank. The dealer was a guy called Fat Harry, who did his business on the street corner without caring who saw. He knew nobody would have the guts to report him and even if they did the cops would turn a blind eye.

'He's in a lot of trouble,' I said.

'That's obvious,' said my mother.

'His pals owe money as well,' spoke Granny. 'I don't know why he's to take the blame.'

'Because he's the leader.'

'Then leader must be another name for mug,' declared my mother.

★   ★   ★

After that, life was so lonely and boring I wanted to cry but I didn't dare in case my mother noticed and sent me to the dentist. She had this theory that toothache was the only thing that made me cry and I'd never given her much cause to think otherwise. I became so desperate for company I took up with a guy in my class called Morton McEwan, another lonely type. Not that I'd always been a loner. It was just a stage I was going through. Anyway, Morton had good reason for being lonely. He wore thick spectacles which gave him an owlish appearance. He also had a bad case of acne. I didn't like being seen with him though I didn't mind going round to his house. He always had plenty of fags and dirty magazines.

I'd been going with Morton for a few days when my mother informed me that Donald was back.

'Back?' I said, wondering whether to be glad or not. I'd actually given up thinking about him.

'Seems he was hiding out in an old shed and his arm's broken. I reckon it was that Fat Harry done it.'

I immediately felt a strong surge of sympathy for Donald. I thought I'd go round and see him. Then my mother, who must have read my thoughts, said, 'In case you're thinking of going round, Granny says he doesn't want to see anybody.'

My sympathy vanished. 'I wasn't even considering it,' I said.

'Ever think of joining a gang?' I asked Morton as we were leafing through some magazines.

'Not really,' he said.

'I think we should. We can't go on like this for ever.'

'Like what?'

'Like drifting along without any purpose. Before you know it we'll be drawing our old age pension.'

He took off his specs and wiped them on his sleeve.

'My mother wouldn't like it,' he said.

'Your mother wouldn't need to know.'

He put his specs on again, stared into the distance and finally said, 'I'll have to think about it.'

On an impulse I jumped up and said, 'Well, you think about it, but I'm not going to hang around here all day while you do.'

I banged the door behind me feeling an unjustifiable anger for him. Surely I could do better than that.

Outside, the street was empty, apart from an old guy hobbling along with the aid of a stick, and a woman nagging at a kid to hurry up. All the shops were closed except a pub on the corner which I was too young for, even if I had the money to drink. How are folk like me supposed to make anything of ourselves in a place like this, I thought balefully. Of course, the plain fact was that folk like me were supposed to stay in and watch the telly, if they're lucky enough to have one.

'Back already?' said my mother, who was getting dressed for the bingo.

'Why shouldn't I be back? There's nothing for young folk to do here. No wonder they take dope.'

She gave me a sharp look. 'Are you referring to yourself, by any chance?'

'No. Just to young folk in general,' I said.

'If it's something to do you're looking for, there's a pile of dishes in the sink,' she said.

'Forget it,' I said, stamping off to my room. Talking to my mother was like banging my head off a brick wall, painful and without purpose. As soon as she'd gone I washed my face and went round to Granny's.

'I heard Donald's back,' I said when she opened the door.

'Yes, and in some state too. He says his arm's broken. I told him to go to a doctor but – '

'Will it be all right if I go up and see him?' I asked. 'Do you think he'd mind?'

'Oh, I'm sure he wouldn't,' she said. 'You go up anyway. I know he's fond of you.'

'Is he?' I said, wondering what made her think that when he'd never given me any hint of it. I ran up the stairs joyfully.

Donald sat on the edge of his bed strumming the guitar, with no sign of a bandage even.

'I thought you had a broken arm,' I said. He stopped strumming and sighed as if I had interrupted him in the middle of some composing.

'No, but it felt like it. I got kicked, you know.' He put his guitar down and asked what I wanted.

'I only came to see if you were OK but if you want me to go – '

He sighed again. 'Actually, I was thinking of topping myself.'

'You were?' I said, not really surprised.

'I might as well do it and save Fat Harry the bother.'

'What about Granny?' I said. 'Wouldn't she lend you something?'

'How could she? She's only got her pension.'

'True,' I said.

We sat for a while, thinking. Then I got an idea so good I couldn't believe it.

'Listen,' I said. 'I know for a fact she's paying up an insurance policy for her funeral. Why don't you ask her to cash it in and tell her if she doesn't it could be your funeral.'

He stared at me thoughtfully through narrowed eyes.

'That's a great idea. I'll ask her as soon as she comes up with the tea. But maybe it's best you should go. She might not want to discuss it in front of anybody. You know what women are like, very secretive.'

The following evening the gang were all there, including Marian. She gave me a hostile glance which I returned with an equally hostile one. Donald told me to hurry up and close the door: did I want the whole world to know his business? I didn't like the way he spoke but before I could dwell on it he was calling for everyone's attention. I waited, thinking he was going to explain how he'd soon be able to pay Fat Harry. Instead, he was saying that Fat Harry was willing to reduce the debt if they all did a bit of collecting for him. Apparently there were so many people owing him money he couldn't keep up with it. There was a silence until Marian declared it was OK with her. I thought that was pretty stupid, considering nobody would expect her to collect. However, that seemed to do the trick. They all agreed that it was OK by them. When I asked Donald later on if this was a wise move he said maybe not but it was the only way he could pay off the debt.

'What about Granny's insurance policy? I thought you were going to ask her – '

'I was, but then I thought she'll need it for her funeral so I didn't bother.'

He turned away then began to talk to Marian as if he'd suddenly found her totally interesting. I thought it was time to leave. No one was speaking to me anyway.

A few days later my mother told me Granny had cashed in her insurance policy to pay for Donald's debt. I was eating cornflakes at the time and I could feel my face flushing, but she didn't seem to notice for she went on, 'To think she's been paying it up all these years and now she'll have nothing for her funeral. I don't know who's going to pay.'

'Maybe the social will pay,' I said, with my head bent low over the plate.

'Maybe they will and maybe they won't,' she snapped. 'All I know is that I can't.'

After that she became so angry about the whole affair that she stopped visiting Granny. She said she was liable to do something drastic to Donald if she ever ran into him.

'So where have you been lately?' asked Morton as were about to watch *Ghostbusters* on video once again.

'Nowhere special. Just hanging around.'

He offered me a cigarette from a silver case containing five. I was quite impressed with it, then he said, 'Watch out for my ma coming in. She always likes to check up on me every so often.'

I smoked the cigarette hurriedly though I suspected it wasn't the smoking that bothered her. It was likely me. She'd a habit of staring at me very suspiciously as if I was up to something. Perhaps she thought I was gay, or we were both gay. I wouldn't have been surprised if Morton was gay by the way he carried on.

'Anyway,' he said, 'I'm glad you came.'

Then a good thing happened to us for a change. We joined up with a bunch of boys a year or so younger than us. They were right into breaking windows and wrecking fences, things like that, nothing drastic except maybe for the time we set the bins alight and all the old folk were out in their shirt-tails. Not that I'd call that drastic. Nobody was burned and anyway some of these old folk had it coming, the way they went on about us playing ball in the street. Though sometimes I felt all this vandalizing was a bit beneath us. I told this to Morton and he said at least we weren't into mugging anybody.

'Not yet,' I said with a laugh.

'I hope you're not in with that lot that's pestering all the neighbours,' my mother was saying when I was on my way out the door. I turned to her indignantly.

'You know I only go round to Morton's to watch videos, but if you like, I'll bring him round here and then you'll know where I am.'

I knew my mother couldn't be bothered having anyone in the house. The effort of trying to put on a pleasant face in front of strangers was always too much for her.

'Don't bother,' she said. 'This place is too big a mess to bring anyone into.'

Then Donald was the main topic with my mother once again. She'd heard in the Co-operative that he'd been arrested for being in possession of drugs.

'I knew it would come to this,' she moaned. 'It was the company he kept. They were a bad influence.'

When I reminded her how she'd once said Donald was the bad influence, she replied that she didn't remember saying anything of the kind but anyway I'd better not turn out like him or she'd put me out.

'Give us break. I've not done anything.'

'Not yet,' she said darkly, then she went on, 'Why don't you go round to see Granny. She's bound to be taking this badly.'

'Why don't you?' I said, for I didn't fancy listening to all that moaning and groaning that would go on about Donald. I could see myself slipping up to his room and strumming his guitar just to get away from it all, and that would be quite a depressing thing to do under the circumstances.

Donald did two months in jail. He came home one day and told Granny he was going to get a job down south as there was nothing doing up here and he would only get into more trouble if he stayed. Granny was quite upset at that. She said she would rather he got into trouble up here because if he got into trouble down south she wouldn't know anything about it. I was sorry to see him go. Having been in jail, he'd become something of a hero to the young lads in the street and I'd hoped some of the glory would rub onto me if we were seen together. Only my mother was pleased. Out of sight, out of mind, she said to Granny, who'd never stopped crying about him for days. It turned out that he never went south after all. We discovered he was living in another part of town with a guy who had a character as bad as Fat Harry's, if not worse.

'I might have known,' said my mother. 'We should be seeing him back any day now to upset us all.'

But he never came and things were altering for me again. It started with the weather becoming colder and some of the young guys not showing up in the evenings. They said they were staying in to study for their exams, which I could hardly believe. Then Morton said he was going to stay in for a spell as his mother didn't want him going out in the fog in case he got done in. What fog, I wondered.

Aloud I said, 'Maybe she's got a point there. I might as well stay in myself and do a bit of studying. It's the only way to get on, I'm thinking.'

I stayed in but I didn't do any studying. Mainly I sat in front of the television hoping to see something of a sexual nature. I liked when my mother went out to the bingo so that I could watch whatever I wanted to without her switching it off.

'You're a funny one,' she would say. 'First you're never in and then you're never out. There's no happy medium with you.'

When I told her that I'd go out in the summer, she said we could all be dead and buried by that time and I said I hoped so.

*　　*　　*

It's April now and the nights are much clearer, which gives me this feeling that I want to go out and kick a ball straight through somebody's window. Still, I've heard some good news today. My mother told me that Donald was seen in the street driving a car. She thinks it's stolen. I asked her if he'd been to see Granny yet and she said she wouldn't be surprised as he's got the cheek for anything.

'And I don't want you going round there,' she added. 'He's a bad influence. I've always maintained that.'

'Don't worry. I wouldn't dream of it,' I said.

As soon as she leaves for the bingo I'm going round to Granny's. Who knows, Donald might be up in his room strumming his guitar. And if he's not there I'll check on the street corner. He's bound to be somewhere near at hand and he might even be glad to see me now I'm a lot older.

PEOPLE LIKE THAT

Mary sat on a bench at the top end of the central station, panicking. Her mind had gone blank again. She knew this was part of her problem, but it was a horrible feeling, as if a brick wall had shut out half her brain. For a minute she couldn't think why she was here then thankfully it came back to her. She was waiting for her son Brian to arrive on the Manchester train due in at platform 10, according to the chap in the ticket-office. It was terrible the way her memory kept going. She was not old enough to have senile dementia. She was only forty-six and it had been like that for two years now. A woman joined her on the seat, keeping to the farther end of it. Mary thought she would ask her about the train in case the chap in the ticket-office had got it wrong.

'Do you happen to know if the Manchester train is running on time? I didnae see it up on the board.'

The woman looked around. 'I'm sure I don't know,' she said, her fat face quite petulant. She had on a pale-blue shiny coat, the kind that Mary associated with those worn by older women at weddings. She didn't like the look of this woman at all but being so nervous and jumpy and alone, she felt compelled to tell the woman that she was meeting her son off the Manchester train and though he had a good job down there, he always liked to come up for a holiday whenever he got the chance because, she added appealingly, 'There's no place like home, is there?'

'Really,' said the woman, looking straight ahead. Mary coughed and settled back on the bench, staring at her wrist and surprised to see no watch on it. She must have left it behind in her hurry to get away. It had been a present from one of the staff too. Well, they could keep it for all she cared, and anyway there was a clock hanging from a pole facing platform 10, so there was no need to worry about the time. All the same, she began to get a bit uptight when she noticed the woman put on a pair of grey kid gloves then begin stroking the backs of them, one hand with another, as though they were pet mice.

'Do you mind not doing that,' said Mary.

'What do you mean?' said the woman, her eyes bulging with indignation as she stared hard at Mary.

'Well, you see it reminds me of the time Brian had his gerbils. He used to stroke them like the way you're doing. Then one day he squashed them, accidentally, mind you. He wouldn't do it deliberately. My Brian was always good with animals – '

The woman broke in. 'If you don't mind, I don't want to hear any more about your Brian.' Then she looked behind her as if expecting to see someone she knew.

78

'I'm sorry if I've offended you,' said Mary. 'It's just that Brian cried so hard about his gerbils.'

'This is too much,' said the woman. She stood up and stamped off down the terrazzo-tiled floor of the station, her heels clicking like castanets. Perplexed, Mary watched her go, wondering what she'd said to annoy this woman with a face like a pig and legs as thick as tree trunks. Likely she was off her head. You were bound to meet people like that in a railway station. That pale-blue coat she had was a ridiculous colour for a woman of her age. Thinking about clothes made Mary wonder if Brian would be ashamed when he saw how she was dressed. Her coat was warm and comfortable but she'd had it for ages, and as for her boots (she reflected, stretching her legs out), the tops were as wrinkled as concertinas, even though she had bought them only two years ago. She frowned. Something else had happened two years ago – something of importance. She was sure it would come to her sometime. She asked a passing porter if the Manchester train was due soon. 'Any minute now,' he said, giving her a suspicious glance. When the train arrived at platform 10 she was standing in front of it, calm and smiling. People came spilling out through the doors but no one who looked like Brian. On the other hand he might have altered a lot since he'd left home, grown taller or fatter, maybe. Her heart leapt when she noticed one young man coming towards her who might possibly be him. He had the same longish chin and colour of hair, though his was worn shorter than Brian's but it was quite possible he'd had it cut by now.

'Excuse me,' she said, standing in front of him. 'Are you Brian McGuire?'

'Shove off,' he said, his face red and indignant.

She stared after him, humiliated. It was terrible the way she got everything wrong nowadays. Come to think of it, that fellow had been nothing near as good-looking as Brian, even allowing for slight changes. Within minutes the people had dispersed and she was left standing on the empty platform. The driver pulled down his window to look at her curiously.

'Can you tell me when the next train arrives in from Manchester?' she asked him. 'You see, I expected my son to be on the one that just came in, but he must have missed it.'

'It's not due for another three hours,' said the driver, 'and it won't come into this platform. As a matter of fact, this one is now going to Greenock.'

'Greenock,' said Mary, her face brightening. 'I believe I've been there once. It's rather a nice place as far as I can remember.'

'Is it?' said the driver, pulling his window back up while she suddenly remembered it was Ayr that she was thinking of. She'd taken Brian there on his twelfth birthday. She remembered how he'd sat tight-lipped and sullen on the journey because she'd snatched the packet of cigarettes out of his hand before they'd stepped onto the train.

'It doesn't look right smoking in front of your mother at your age,' she'd told him. 'You'll get them back when we get there.'

'Aye, and that's a whole two fuckin' hours away,' he'd said.

On looking back she saw it as a good day. Brian had spent all his time in the amusements when he wasn't lighting up fags, while she had sat on a seat on the esplanade looking out on a stormy sea. After that she'd taken a walk along the beach where the sand blew into her eyes. Still, it had been May so what could she expect. Anyway, the cold wind had made her all the more appreciative of the warm café where she ordered tea and scones. Brian had stood outside eating a fish supper. He wouldn't be seen dead in a dump like that, he'd explained. She sighed with regret that he was too old to take anywhere now and even apart from that she knew he preferred being with his pals. She began to wonder what she could do to pass the time. Perhaps she should go for a cup of tea if Wimpy's was still open. Her hand searched inside her coat pocket for the pound coin she had amongst some change. She might even manage to buy herself a cake. It was such a nuisance that she had lost track of what things cost nowadays. She was walking in what she hoped was the right direction for Wimpy's when she saw in the distance the woman in the pale-blue coat talking to a porter and pointing in her direction. Mary panicked. Was the woman complaining about something, saying she'd been sworn at, or worse still, assaulted? This had happened to her before on a chance encounter with another crazy bitch who'd said Mary had tried to steal her purse, which was a downright lie, nevertheless she had ended up in court charged with attempted theft, and fined. Don't let it happen again, she prayed. Luckily the Ladies was only a few yards away. She nipped into it quickly down a few stairs then through a turnstile marked OUT OF ORDER.

'Ten pence, please,' called the attendant.

Mary turned back and threw a few coins on the counter which she was sure was more than enough but she had no time to count them in case the woman in the blue coat was following her. Inside the cubicle she waited for at least ten minutes. By the time she came back up into the station there was no sign of the woman. The place was strangely deserted except for a few people sitting or standing here and there. Perhaps they'd nowhere else to go, thought Mary. At least she had a reason to be here. She began to wander down past the shops on the left-hand side of the station, all closed but their windows displaying articles which Mary considered were trash. Imagine paying five pounds for a tie and worse, forty pounds for a thick, ugly string of beads no better than the ones her mother used to keep in a chest. The coffee house, still open, was more interesting in its own way with its delicious smell of coffee wafting through the door. But she would never have gone in there even if she could have afforded it. It was much too snobbish looking. She would have been very much out of place. The Wimpy bar was closed when she came to it so she went back up to the kiosk that sold newspapers and chocolate, thinking a Milky Way would do her fine, and discovering it was closed too. She saw a man standing at the side of the kiosk wearing a long fawn raincoat and drinking out of a dark bottle. She glanced at him without meaning to as she walked past but something about him made her stop and turn back. The man took the bottle away from his mouth.

'Hey, whit are ye lookin' at?'

Bleary-eyed and unshaven though he was, Mary thought she recognized him. The more she looked at him, the angrier he became.

'You want a punch on the face or somethin'?'

It dawned on her who it could be. Of course she mustn't jump to conclusions.

'Pardon me,' she said, 'but do you happen to be Brian McGuire who used to live with his wife Mary along in Young Street twenty years ago, though I expect the place is not there now and – '

'What the fuck are you on about?' he said, wiping the side of his mouth.

She could have slapped his face at the rotten way he spoke to her, but then even in those early days he had been a foul-mouthed drunkard.

'I'm Mary, your wife.'

'Mary,' he repeated, as if this information was no surprise. He held out the bottle. 'Dae ye want some of this?'

'No thanks, I only usually have a port and lemon.'

The last time she had a port and lemon was on Christmas Day with two of the staff. It was funny how she could remember that. Yet she couldn't remember the important things, like what the thing was that had happened two years ago.

'Don't be so bloody sarcastic when I'm only tryin' to be civil,' said the drunk whose name she was convinced was Brian McGuire.

'Do you know,' she told him, 'you've got a son who's coming up in the Manchester train. Don't you think you should go and meet him?'

Even as she said this she couldn't see Brian pleased to find this man was his father. The drunk man puffed his cheeks and shook his head as if all this information was getting him down. He thrust the bottle in front of her face.

'Better take some o' that. You need it mair than I dae.'

This time Mary accepted the bottle, wiping it first with the rim of her coat sleeve before she put it to her mouth.

'Anyway,' said the drunk, 'my wife's name wis Nan and she's been deid a long time so it's no' possible.'

'Would you like to see Brian's photo?' asked Mary, fumbling inside her dress. The drunk held up a hand in warning.

'Don't try pinnin' anything on me. I've nae son.'

Mary didn't answer. Her attention was taken up by the sight of a policeman heading in their direction. The drunk must have seen him too for he shoved the bottle in his coat pocket and moved hastily towards the taxi rank. Blindly, she followed him and the next thing she was out on the busy street but not for long. When he veered without warning to his left, she discovered she was in a dark alley enclosed on each side by tall buildings. Unable to see very well, she groped her way along the wall thinking that the drunk man, who might not be her husband after all, would be gone by now, but when she touched his face as he stood inside a doorway, she realized he'd been waiting for her all along. He grabbed her wrist.

'Right, whit's your game?'

'I've no game. I only wanted to get away from that policeman.'

He laughed. 'You're a hoor then. Is that it?'

'I told you already, I was waiting on my son coming off the Manchester train.'

The drunk swore under his breath then asked her if she had any money. She told him that she'd only a few coins but when he pulled her towards him and began to put his hands all over her body, she gave him the pound coin she'd been clutching ever since she left the station.

'Christ, that'll no' get much,' he said savagely, peering at it in the palm of his hand. 'And you'd the bloody cheek to take some o' ma drink.'

He took the bottle out of his pocket, emptied what was in it down his throat then smashed it against the wall. Mary was frightened to move in case the glass went through the sole of her boot but that consideration was soon forgotten when she was slammed back against the wall.

'Scream and I'll throttle ye,' said the drunk as he wrenched her coat open. Mary heard the buttons she had newly sewn on that morning rattling along the cobblestones as a flaccid penis was thrust in her hand. 'Pull it,' he demanded. Mary did her best to comply in the hope he would let her go all the sooner but nothing happened. It was like flogging a dead horse, she thought. Her arm was getting tired.

'See you,' he said, thrusting it off, 'you're nae fuckin' use. Try gi'en it the kiss o' life.'

When Mary refused absolutely he pulled up her dress and said, 'Is this whit ye want?'

Then he began to pump away at her as though his life depended on it. Mary's head hit the wall and as if this jolt had done the trick she remembered suddenly that Brian had died of an overdose two years ago when he'd gone down to Manchester with his junkie friends. 'There's nothin' to dae up here,' had been his excuse.

'Oh, my poor Brian,' she said aloud, wanting to cry but unable to do so with the man's weight crushing against her.

'Never mind poor Brian. Think o' me for a change,' said the drunk. After what seemed like an eternity, he gave a shudder and became still. It seemed to be over. He must have had some success yet she expected a blow on the mouth. Her husband had always done that. However, the drunk, who was fumbling with the zip on his trousers, only said, 'Another thing. Ma name's Ronnie, no' Brian, so ye can rest assured I'm definitely no' the man yer lookin' for,' then he walked away into the dark.

Mary made sure he was gone before she went back to the station, with the smell of him in her nostrils which she suspected might never go away. A man and woman came forward to meet her as she headed for platform 10.

'Right Mary,' said the woman taking a hold of her arm, 'there's no need to go any farther. You're coming back with us.'

The man took her other arm. Both their grips were gentle but firm.

'You're a bad girl giving us such a hard time trying to find you. Where have you been?'

'I was waiting for the Manchester train.'

'One of these days you're going to come to real harm, you know,' said the woman, now putting her own arm through Mary's like a close friend would.

As they passed the ticket-office the chap behind the window called out, 'I see you've found her.'

'Yes,' said the man. 'I hope we haven't put you to any bother. She's a sad case really.'

'No bother at all,' said the railway clerk. 'We have them in here all the time – people like that.'

THE MARIGOLD FIELD

After telling me she was going to take a holiday in the Bahamas, my sister Celia thrust a black and white snapshot under my nose.

'Do you remember this?' she said.

I glanced at it. 'Not really.' Then I asked her if she could afford it.

'You mean the holiday? Of course I can.' She stared back at the photo. 'You must remember. It's the one Father took of us in the marigold field.'

I glanced at it again. 'So it is. Don't we look awful?'

Celia considered it, frowning. 'I think we look OK. That was the style, in those days. You can't compare them with now.'

'It wasn't the style. We wore cast-offs even at school. I was always ashamed.'

'I don't remember. I'm sure Mother did her best.'

'I'm not blaming Mother,' I said. 'Father never gave her enough for clothes.'

I took back the photo and studied it. Celia and I had dresses with frills round the hems that hung well below our knees while Hughie, our four-year-old brother, wore a jumper with a polo-neck covering his chin.

I pointed this out to Celia. 'A jumper in the summer? It's ridiculous.'

'That's because he always caught colds summer and winter.' She added grudgingly, 'How is he by the way?'

'Fine.' I wasn't going to elaborate on Hughie's lifestyle. Celia was bound to blame Mother for it. She always had.

'I can't imagine him being fine.'

'Well, he manages like everybody else.'

'Surely not like everybody else?' she said laughingly and then became serious 'Why did we call it the marigold field? There wasn't a single marigold in it. I looked often enough.'

'It was Mother who called it that. She got the name out of a book.'

To change the subject I asked if she was going on holiday alone.

'God, no. I'm going with Dickie.'

She explained that Dickie was old enough to be her father but had plenty of money and that was the main thing. I said I was glad to hear at least one of the family was doing well. She looked hard at me, perhaps for a sign of irony, then said I could come with them if I liked. Dickie had always wanted to meet me. I thanked her and said I'd rather not. I wouldn't like to spoil their holiday.

'Whatever you think,' she said with a tight smile which I suspected was one of relief. Looking at the photo over my shoulder, she added, 'I wonder if the dam Father made is still there?'

'Dam?' I said, then after a pause, 'You mean the one where he tried to drown Hughie?'

She gave me a sharp look. 'Surely you still don't believe that after all this time?'

'Oh, yes, I believe it. I saw him, didn't I?'

It had been exceptionally warm that day in the marigold field. Celia had said she wished the stream was deep enough to swim in. Father, who always liked being busy, began to dam it up with stones and mud until a wide pool appeared. Celia flung off her clothes and jumped in with her knickers on. 'Come on,' she called out. 'This is terrific.' With one eye on Father, who stood on the bank close to Hughie, I undid my sandals. Suddenly my brother was floundering in the water like a drowning pup. I screamed when I saw his head go under. I didn't know what to do and apparently neither did Father. He simply stood there looking down. It was Celia who pulled Hughie up, spluttering and choking and purple in the face. I'm sure if it hadn't been for her he would have drowned. Undoubtedly I was relieved that Hughie was safe. What nagged my brain was that a second before he fell I had seen Father's hand on his shoulder. I told Celia this when nobody else was listening. She said, 'What is that supposed to mean?' I said it meant Father had pushed him.

Mother, who had been sitting under a tree, came running up to ask what had happened. 'The sun was so hot I must have fallen asleep,' she explained. When it dawned on her Hughie had nearly drowned she shrieked and clasped him to her, stifling his sobs so that he appeared to be smothering. Later, I plucked up courage to tell her I'd seen Father push Hughie into the pool but she said I had imagined it and I had read too many trashy books.

And now Celia was saying, 'I don't know how many times I've asked this before but why on earth would Father want to drown his only son, for God's sake?'

I felt my temper rising. 'You don't seem to understand. A father can be as jealous of his son as he can be of a lover. Gorillas are known to kill their sons from jealousy and they are as near human as you'll get.'

'You can't compare Father to a gorilla,' said Celia. 'And what was there to be jealous of? Hughie was always a weakling. How could anybody be jealous of him?'

'Weakling or not,' I shouted, 'Mother loved Hughie best. That's why Father was jealous! I don't think you ever knew what Father was like.'

'And you did,' she sneered. I could see she was upset.

'Let's forget it,' I said. 'I shouldn't have brought it up.'

At the same time I blamed Celia. If she hadn't shown me the photo I would never have opened my mouth. To hide my rancour I asked her if she was considering getting married.

'I might,' she said. 'I wouldn't like to end up an old maid.'

When I said that perhaps marriage wasn't everything, she replied that maybe it wasn't but it was better to find that out for oneself. As we parted on the doorstep I had the feeling we might not see each other again.

'I hope everything goes well for you,' I called out as she was going down the path. She turned round.

'You too, and give my regards to Hughie.'

'I will,' I shouted back with all the sincerity I could muster, though I hadn't seen Hughie for weeks and didn't want to. It was a pity, I thought, that Celia and I had never met without quarrelling after Mother died. As children we had been very close.

But Mother had left the house and furniture to me. I would rather have had the sum of money which Celia and Hughie had received but it was no use telling Celia that. She said I'd always been Mother's favourite so what could she expect? I pointed out that Hughie was Mother's favourite and she'd left me the house to ensure he'd always have a roof above his head. She'd made me promise that I'd never sell it while he was alive. Celia then said if Hughie had been Mother's favourite why did she let him smoke the stub ends of her roll-ups from the time he was ten years old?

'Maybe she never knew,' I said.

'She knew all right. She just didn't care.'

I couldn't argue. Mother had smoked dope from the day she married, or so I gathered from an aunt who came to her funeral and said that was why Father had left us. He couldn't stand having a dope addict for a wife. This didn't stop me loving her, not even when she began taking stronger stuff than hash. I could never condemn her. She was like a child with her small delicate bones and pale skin. Sometimes, if she was in a good mood, she let me brush her long flaxen hair and tilted her head backwards and closed her eyes. In a few years her face grew as lined as an old woman's, her hair fell out and she was obliged to wear a wig.

'Her arms are all holes,' said Celia. 'I don't know how she can do that to herself.'

The word 'Hughie' sprang to mind but I didn't say it.

'Perhaps she's a diabetic,' I said. 'I'm sure she attends a clinic.'

Celia gave me a look as if to say, 'How can you be so stupid?'

When Father left us (I was never sure why in those days) we stopped going to the marigold field. Mother said she couldn't bear to go back to that place where she had once been so happy. I was surprised at this. I didn't think any of us had been all that happy with Father continually nagging at us.

'Say cheese,' he'd ordered when taking the photo. We said cheese but it didn't seem to cheer us up. 'You're the most miserable kids I've ever seen,' he told us. 'I don't know what's the matter with you. Can't any of you smile for a change?'

For years Mother maintained it was because of me Father had left.

'He couldn't stand being accused of trying to drown Hughie in the marigold field.'

'I never actually accused him,' I said. 'I only mentioned it to you and Celia.'

'Well, that's as good as being accused,' she'd said, picking up a shoe and throwing it at me. It missed. This was the beginning of her violent period. Celia and I started keeping out of her way and it was Hughie who kept her company. Of course he had his reasons. Mother always gave him money and because of that we had to live on very little. Sometimes there was only bread and margarine to eat but Mother didn't seem to mind, nor did Hughie. I sometimes listened outside her bedroom door to find out if they were talking about me, saying that I had driven Father away, things like that, but all I ever heard was an occasional shriek of laughter.

One day when he was leaving her room I said to him, 'Don't you know you're killing her with that stuff you both take?'

He shook his head and said, 'I'm keeping her alive more than any doctor would.'

'If the state she's in is being alive then perhaps she'd be better off dead.'

'Is that what you want?' he asked, staring at me blankly. At that moment I thought his resemblance to Mother was striking, perhaps because of their expressions.

'I want my mother back,' I said, 'not that stranger in there.'

'Then you shouldn't have forced Father out. That was her problem.'

'I never forced Father out. He left because he couldn't stand any of us. He tried to drown you in the burn when you were a child.'

'So you keep telling me,' he said, walking off with a jaunty swing to his hips which meant Mother had given him money.

All that seems a long time ago, though to be honest I've lost track of time. Was it last year or the year before that Celia paid me a visit before she went on holiday? I can't remember clearly and not having heard anything, I picture her living in the Bahamas for ever with an old man at her side who resembles Father. Funnily enough I dream about Father quite a lot. I don't know why for he's not on my conscience any more. I'm beginning to believe he left because of Mother's addiction, and it was nothing to do with me or Hughie.

With everyone gone the house is so silent you could hear a pin drop, though within that silence I sometimes imagine I hear voices whispering in Mother's room. It's probably the wind. But when I go outside it's usually quite calm and this disturbs me. I can't sleep very well and jump at the least thing. Tomorrow I will put the house in the hands of an estate agent. Since Hughie died there's no need to keep a roof for him. He went quite suddenly. The certificate mentioned pneumonia but I suspect Mother's death was the cause. Without her he had no reason to live.

When cleaning out the drawers in readiness for departure I came across the photo Father took of us in the marigold field. My first thought was to have it enlarged and framed, as I had intended when Celia left it with me. But now I see the edges are curled and the surface is cracked. It's a pity because it would have looked nice on the mantelpiece of my new home. On second thoughts this may not be advisable. It would be a reminder of the past and I don't think I need that or even want it.

I was about to tear it up before putting it in the bin with the other rubbish when I suddenly remembered Mother saying that it was bad luck to destroy a photograph. Though not superstitious I dislike taking chances. There's been enough bad luck in the family. I'll keep it in the drawer until I can face it without a qualm. Otherwise I'll leave it there until it crumbles into dust.

INTRUDERS

Nobody lived in the terrace any more apart from an old man who'd refused to leave when it had been condemned. Then one night tinkers crept in for shelter and stayed for ages. There was also a boy who hung around the crumbling doorways sniffing glue. Nobody worried about these folk. The authorities knew they'd shift when the bulldozer moved in.

Entering a room whose only furniture was a table and two chairs left by the previous owner, George the tinker asked his wife, 'Where is she then?'

'If it's Greta yer talkin' aboot,' said Flora, 'Ah dinnae ken. She was away when Ah got up.'

'Whit time was that?'

'Ah'm no' sure. Whit difference dis it make?'

'Nane.'

George lifted his tobacco-tin with an air of exhaustion. He'd drunk too much the night before and doubted if he'd feel better before he drank some more but the bottle on the table was empty. After watching him make a very thin roll-up Flora gestured to a heap of ash in the grate.

'Mibby you could see yer way to bringin' in wood for a fire afore we freeze to death.' She pointed to the child under a heap of blankets in a big pram. 'If ye don't, how wull Ah heat his milk?'

'Give it to him cauld,' said George, who had forgotten to chop up logs the night before but didn't want to admit it. He offered his wife the roll-up. She refused.

'If he takes it cauld he'll get a chill.'

'He usually takes it cauld,' said George, closing his eyes to blot out his wife's accusing face.

He opened them when she poked his arm saying, 'Mibby she's gone tae Maggie's.'

'Who's gone tae Maggie's?'

'Greta, you fool.'

He thought for a minute then said, 'Maggie's is miles away.'

'She could've got a lift.'

'And somethin' else beside,' he said darkly.

'Greta can look efter hersel'. She's nearly sixteen,' said Flora though inwardly angered as well as worried by her daughter's disappearance. Greta had been good with the child. 'Onyway,' she added, 'Ah widnae be surprised if she's got money for the fares. You know whit she's like.'

'Naw. Whit's she like?'

'You know as well as Ah dae that she's good at the cadgin', with her being so pretty and well spoken like Ah wis masel' once.'

George gave a harsh laugh. 'That must have been afore ma time.'

Flora's anger flared up as the child began to whimper. 'You'd better get that fire goin'. The bairnie's cauld.'

'He's no sae much cauld as hungry,' said George. 'Gie him somethin' tae eat.'

Flora spread some jam on a slice of bread and gave it to the child, who immediately stopped whimpering as if to prove his father's point.

'Ah telt ye he wis hungry,' said George, adding quickly when he saw the look on Flora's face, 'Ah'll fetch the logs as soon as Ah smoke this fag.'

'Ah'm no' waitin',' said Flora, blowing on her hands then rubbing them together. 'Ah'm gaun tae lie under the blankets ben the room. It's the only way Ah'll get a heat.'

'Me too,' said George. 'Ah could dae with a right cosy kip.'

'You're stayin' here tae look efter him. He'll no want tae lie doon noo he's wakened and he cannae be left by hissel'.' As an afterthought she added that maybe they should take a walk later to look for Greta.

'Ah thought you said she'd likely be at Maggie's?'

'There's nae herm in lookin',' said Flora. With that she was off into a back room leaving George staring after her resentfully.

Two hours later they walked along the pavement with Flora pushing the pram. The child could easily have walked but pushing him was less trouble. When they reached the Rowantree Inn she suggested that they buy some cans of lager. George frowned as if it hadn't been his intention, then produced some silver from his pocket.

'It so happens Ah might hae enough,' he said, disappearing into the public bar. Minutes later he came out with four cans of lager, three of which he placed in the bottom of the pram. The other they drank between them before setting off. When they reached a side road leading up a hill Flora turned the pram in its direction. George asked her why as it only led to a farm.

'Ah like the smell o' dung.'

Bemused, George scratched his head then said, 'Isn't that the place where they offered me a job once?'

'Which ye didnae take.'

'Well, Ah hope you dinnae think Ah'm takin' it noo,' said George. He drew her attention to the child rolling the cans up and down the pram. 'They're gaun tae be fizzing all over the place when we open them.'

'Stop yer grumblin',' said Flora. 'Yer always grumblin'.'

George reached for a can and she told him to leave it until later.

At the top of the hill they sat on a grassy verge next to the farmhouse wall with the child crushed between them. Flora was drinking from her can when George asked her why, if they were supposed to be looking for Greta, they had come up here.

'Ah'm no sure,' she said. 'Ah thought we might run intae her, but it doesnae seem likely. Mibby she's at Maggie's right enough.'

'So how can ye be sure o' that then?'

'Ah never said Ah wis sure. Ah'm only thinkin' she might

be because she wis aye talkin' aboot her aunt's fine caravan and how could we no' stay wi' her instead o' that dump we're in. That's whit she wis aye sayin'.'

George swallowed some lager. 'Ah don't know how she could say that when she knows fine Ah couldnae staun bein wi' your sister for a single second, fine caravan or no'.'

'Maggie couldnae staun you either but Ah don't doubt she wid have been pleased tae see some o' her kinsfolk. It's no' fair Ah don't get tae visit her because o' you.'

'Because o' me?' said George indignantly. 'You can go and see her ony time ye want.'

At that point the child began to struggle.

'Stop that, ye devil,' said Flora, giving him a nip on the leg which made him sit still. 'Ah think Ah wull go,' she said, resuming the previous subject. 'Ah might as well enjoy masel' for a chinge.'

'Don't forget it takes money,' said George.

'Mibby Ah could get a lift.'

'Who's gaun tae gie you a lift?' said George in a derisive tone. 'Yer no whit ye'd call good-lookin'.'

Flora looked round at him dangerously. 'Whit's that ye said?'

'Ah wis just jokin',' said George hurriedly. 'Ye can be good-lookin' enough when ye want tae.'

He made them each a roll-up. Slightly mollified, Flora took hers then pointed out they could both go to Maggie's when the giro came since by then they'd have the money for fares.

'Mibby,' said George. 'But whit if Greta's no' there? Whit will we dae then?'

'We'll have tae report her missin'.'

She took a sip of lager then spat it out. 'That stuff's rotten,' she said. 'Either that or it's ma stomach.'

George then said that if they reported Greta missing the cops would find they were living in the terrace and boot them out and they'd have nowhere to go.

'So whit can we dae?' said Flora sourly. The dampness of the grass was seeping through her skirt and her stomach felt queasy. The child began struggling again and she put the can to his mouth to shut him up. He pushed it away, spilling the contents. She lost her temper and threw it over the wall, then stood up and almost flung the child into the pram.

'Ah'm gaun back,' she said. 'This place stinks.'

'Hey, wait a minute,' said George. 'There's still a can left.'

'You take it,' said Flora. 'Onyway, Ah've got this funny feelin' Greta could be in by noo and wonderin' where we are.'

'You and your funny feelin's,' said George. 'Ah widnae be surprised if you've gone clean oot yer mind.'

'Neither wid Ah,' said Flora.

In silence they walked back the way they'd come. The child was lulled to sleep with the bumping of the pram. George finished his lager and threw the empty can into a turnip field.

'Ah'll get some o' these turnips later,' he promised.

Flora didn't bother to answer. They were halfway down the terrace lane when they encountered the boy standing in a doorway with a Cellophane bag stuck to his chin.

'God, you gied me a fright,' Flora said to him. 'Whit's that thing on your jaw?'

George said, couldn't she see it was for sniffing glue then asked the boy if he'd seen a girl hanging around the place, pretty and fair-haired. The boy, frightened at being spoken to, ran off.

'Ah dinnae like the look o' him,' said Flora. 'Ah widnae be surprised if he knows somethin'.'

'Like whit?'

'Like where Greta is. Ah'd go efter him if Ah wis you.'

George sighed. The whole business was beginning to give him a headache. He suspected Greta wasn't far away but he wished she was, for she'd been getting on his nerves lately. That last time she'd stolen his money, he'd had to keep his mouth shut about it in case she told Flora what they got up to when she was away for the messages. It would suit him better if she never turned up.

'Let's forget aboot Greta,' he said. 'There's plenty ither things on ma mind.'

'Whit kind o' things?'

'Things like me gettin' in tae the hoose so's Ah can rest ma bones in a chair. Ah dinnae ken whit's wrang wi me this weather but Ah'm always tired.'

'So you want me tae forget ma daughter,' said Flora bitterly. 'Is that whit yer sayin'?'

'She's no' ma daughter,' said George. 'I didnae clap eyes on her until she wis ten.'

Unable to dispute the truth of this, Flora said with mounting fury, 'Ye'll be tellin' me next that bairn in the pram isnae yours either?'

'Ah widnae be surprised if he's no',' said George, taking the pram off her and pushing it along the cobble-stones in a desperate fashion. When they reached the stairs leading to their makeshift home he ordered her to give him a hand up. Sullenly she complied.

Inside the living-room they both sat down on the chairs with their legs apart.

'So she never came back,' said Flora after a while.

George, who'd been about to doze off, opened one eye and said, 'She's probably at Maggie's.'

'Probably,' said Flora. She stared at the grate full of dead ash and was about to ask George to go and fetch in logs but decided against it when he began to snore. He usually got into a rage when awakened suddenly. She'd fetch them in herself. With a sigh she stood up and went outside.

From within a doorway, the boy who'd been sniffing glue saw her cross the lane and go into one of the old wash-houses and wondered if she was looking for the girl. If he hadn't taken fright when they bumped into him earlier he could have explained that he'd seen the girl go up the old man's stairs. Though they might not have believed him. They'd looked at him very suspiciously. In any case it wasn't the first time he'd seen the girl go up the old man's stairs. Maybe it was to clean his house or make him a cup of tea. He couldn't imagine what else it could be. Anyway, it was none of his business what she did and besides, tinkers were always best avoided. They didn't act like normal people. He was thinking these things when someone grabbed him by the back of his jumper.

'Got you,' said a man's voice. 'And sniffing glue as well. You're definitely for it now.'

The boy managed to twist his head round far enough to see the man from the school-board.

'Ah'll come,' said the boy, 'but leave me go.'

The man only tightened his hold on the jumper and frogmarched him down the lane. By that time the tinker girl was clean gone from the boy's mind. He'd too much else to worry about.

LÉONIE

This is an account of a day in the life of Léonie Fabre who lived in a village in Provence. Before the war it had been a good place to stay though the villagers sometimes referred to it as a hole in the ground, encircled as it was by a canyon of rock and overshadowed by a range of mountains. Tourists came to gaze at the mountains and the canyon and most of all the fountain of water that poured from a cleft in the base of the rock, filling a basin in the earth then spilling over to become a fast-flowing river that ran through the centre of the village. But when war broke out no one came except soldiers and foreign officials. The village had become occupied.

On the morning of this particular day Léonie opened the shutters and was dismayed to see that snow had fallen during the night. It was three years since snow had last fallen but she did not welcome it the more for that, especially when she must go to the store for bread and tobacco. Her shoes were unsuitable for walking through snow and she had nothing better to wear. She turned to her husband who sat tapping his pipe on the table.

'I suppose you have no tobacco left?' she asked.

'You have supposed correctly,' he said with a scowl on his dark, lean face. Though middle-aged he appeared much younger, perhaps because of his lithe figure, and his hair which was as black as a raven. His eyes were cold and when he smiled, which was seldom, he did so grudgingly. He was known in the village as a very proud man. Some said he was merely overbearing and conceited because of the land he owned. Most of the villagers owned land but not as much as he. His crops were the finest and even though part of them was confiscated by the foreign officials he still tended them lovingly and diligently. Léonie, though younger than her husband, had aged beyond her years. Her face, pretty at one time, was pinched and marked with lines. Her once light-brown and curling hair had become dingy and lifeless. Her expression had been serene but was now permanently anxious. Those changes had taken place after her son had been drowned on his ninth birthday many years before. They were not caused by the strain of living in an occupied village.

'I suppose you know it is snowing,' she said.

'I know.'

'You are still going to the land then?'

'Where else?'

'I thought perhaps because of the snow – '

'Whether it is snowing or not there is always something to do. Besides I would go out of my mind if I did not get to my land.' He threw her a disparaging glance. 'It is the only thing that gives me any pleasure.'

Léonie plucked at her lips nervously. 'I was thinking that perhaps I might not be able to get any more tobacco from the store. As you know it is rationed and I – '

Her husband answered loudly, 'Then I must go without.'

'On the other hand perhaps if I pay extra Madame Renet will allow me some. It is scarce, you understand, but sometimes she can get it from the black market which means I have to pay extra.'

'In the name of God,' her husband shouted, 'do not tire me with all this talk of tobacco. If you cannot get it for me someone else will and without any fuss either. You should know by this time I depend on you for very little.'

'Yes,' she said vaguely, relieved to hear that the responsibility of his tobacco did not entirely rest with her. She still knew she would have to try the store for it was not certain he would get it from someone else.

She began to speak on a subject that had been on her mind since she had heard about it from Lotz the postman.

'Do you know,' she said, 'I cannot get it out of my head about the Mayor.'

'The Mayor?'

'According to Lotz it appears he has been burned to death in some kind of place called a concentration camp. I was going to tell you last night after you finished your meal. But when you fell asleep I decided it was best not to disturb you. But isn't that terrible if it's true?'

Her husband frowned as he pondered on this. Then he said, 'I doubt that it will be true. Why should they burn a cowardly man like the Mayor who has never shown his face in the village since the occupation began?'

'Lotz said that the foreign officials took him away many months ago and only now has this terrible news been heard. If it is not true why should he tell such a story?'

'Because he is a gossip and a liar like all the others in this village who have nothing else to do than make up tales.'

'But what if it is true?'

'Then if it is true I would say the Mayor has done something to deserve it. He was always a corrupt man and easily bribed. I remember the time he got young Patrice Rouyer out of the village to stand trial in the city after he raped a servant girl and so got off with a light sentence instead of being lynched by the villagers as he deserved. Of course the Rouyer family were rich in those days so the Mayor would have been well paid.'

'I do not recall that,' said Léonie, 'but anyway, Lotz said that the Mayor was burned because his own son is one of those who lives in the mountains.'

Her husband smiled sardonically. 'Oh, well, that would be reason enough to burn the Mayor when his son is one of those who take it upon themselves to blow up a train or a bridge and let innocent people pay the price. But even if Lotz's story is true I am not concerned. I have more important matters to think of.'

He rose from his chair and picked up his jacket from their bed near the fireplace then lifted his parcel of bread and cheese from the dresser and left without saying goodbye.

The moment he had gone Léonie entered the one other room, which had been her son's, and sat on the edge of the bed where he had slept, waiting for what she thought of as his presence. This presence was nothing she could see or touch. Sometimes it was like a warm draught in her face and sometimes like a soft breathing in her ears. Once she actually thought she saw his shape at the foot of the bed but when she reached out with her hand it disappeared. She told no one of this, certainly not her husband, and she never entered this room when her husband was at home. It was her one solace.

In the afternoon she walked along the narrow pavement looking for tracks to follow in the snow. There were none. The street was deserted. Her feet quickly became cold and wet though the snow no longer fell so heavily. A keen wind had sprung up reducing it to a few scattered flakes. She came to the post office and noticed that, though the door was locked, a light shone in the upper window and the postman's bicycle leaned against the wall. She would have liked to speak to Lotz, and ask if the story of the Mayor being burned had perhaps only been a rumour, but it was not advisable to wait. If the foreign officials came by in their car they might stop and question her. Besides, it was too cold to hang about so she walked on, passing the Mayor's villa on a shelf of rock high above the other houses, stone stairs leading up to the porch. The shutters of the windows were closed. There was nothing to suggest it was occupied, not even a wisp of smoke from the chimneys. The Mayor's face came into her head, sad and inconsolable. She shook her head to be rid of it then turned a corner and crossed the bridge over the river that had taken her son, and for once wasn't aware of it. She scarcely glanced at the soldier on guard outside the town hall, though he was resplendent in black boots, long army coat and steel helmet, with rifle resting on shoulder. To the villagers he represented a situation that had become stale for everyone.

In sight of the grocery store she saw Agnès Duval approaching, as thin as a screwdriver in a long, tight-fitting, black coat, her head bare, her greasy hair flapping in the wind. Léonie would have preferred to avoid Agnès. She was known to be slightly mad but not as mad as her brother, an arsonist. Long before the occupation he had fled to the city after setting fire to the local paper-mill when the owners refused him a job. Some people said he had joined the resistance, others reported him to be in pay of the enemy. Either way he was credited with many desperate deeds.

'Good day' said Léonie, hoping to move on quickly, but Agnès stopped immediately in front of her, saying, 'What is so good about it? There is nothing to be obtained in the store, yet the owner is as fat as a pig. What does she expect me to do – eat grass or worms? Well, I won't have it. Soon I am going to the city where everyone eats meat. This village has gone to the dogs now that the socialists have taken over.'

With that she spat on the snow and moved off rapidly down the pavement, talking to herself. Léonie entered the store shaking her arms to get rid of the snow on her coat.

'Be careful,' said Madame Renet from behind her counter. She was a stout woman with eyes as black as currants in her pale, puffy face. She pointed to a box of cauliflowers lying on the floor. 'I do not want them damaged. They are very expensive.'

Then she came round from her counter and began to brush imaginary snow from the vegetables.

'I am sorry,' said Léonie. 'The snow is everywhere. It is difficult to avoid.'

'I know,' said Madame Renet, 'but I have to keep an eye on these vegetables. They are not easy to obtain.'

'You say they are expensive?' said Léonie, eyeing the cauliflowers wistfully. It was a long time since she had seen one. They were not grown in the village. She considered them too beautiful to eat. If she could have bought one she would have kept it in water until it rotted.

'They are,' said the shopkeeper. 'I could not even afford one for myself.'

'And who could?' said Léonie absently.

'You would be surprised who could.'

'The foreign officials, or the soldiers perhaps?'

'Not only them. The priest can afford them just as he can afford everything else that is too dear for the villagers.'

'Really?'

'But what can I do. I must sell my stock.'

'Of course,' agreed Léonie, adding, 'But what can you expect of a priest. He is used to having the best.'

'I tell you what I expect,' said Madame Renet, folding her arms over her chest. 'I expect if he was a good priest he would have spoken out against the enemy instead of sending his housekeeper round to this store to buy all the luxuries that no one else can afford.'

'It is dangerous to speak out against the enemy. He could get shot for that.'

'Then I would expect him to get shot.'

Léonie was uncomfortable with the subject. She had

never attended church since her son died. She did not want to talk about the priest, though she recollected vaguely he was a young man who had come from a village far south in the region. She'd heard his sermons were more concerned with God's wrath than his forgiveness but though he was not liked on that account he was respected for his fervour.

She said, 'Since I do not go to church I do not expect anything.'

Madame Renet raised her eyebrows. 'I am surprised at that. I always go to church for I pray to God, not the priest.'

Léonie kept silent for a while then said, looking round the shop, 'Has the bread van not yet arrived?'

'I am afraid not and I doubt it will with the roads being so bad.'

Taking a deep breath Léonie asked, 'I was wondering if you have any tobacco to sell. My husband is quite desperate for some.'

With a pained expression the shopkeeper turned round and took a black book from the shelf behind her then placed it on the counter and leafed through it slowly. She stopped halfway down a page and said, 'It is marked here that your husband had two ounces a fortnight ago.'

Léonie stared at the book but could make nothing out since it was upside-down.

'A fortnight is a long time,' she said.

'I am sorry,' said Madame Renet. 'Tobacco is very scarce. I have to make sure everyone receives an equal ration.'

'I will pay you extra.'

'Extra!' said the woman as if scandalized, then, 'How much?'

'One franc.'

Madame Renet shook her head regretfully.

'All right, two,' said Léonie, judging she could afford it when there was no bread to buy.

'Very well then,' said Madame Renet with a sigh. 'I will see what I can do since your husband is so desperate.'

She brought out a packet of tobacco from under the counter then placed it on the top. Léonie took two francs from her coat pocket and handed them over. The transaction completed, she said as if it had just come into her head, 'Have you heard the news about the Mayor?'

'I have,' said Madame Renet, again folding her arms across her chest and looking grim.

'So it is true he was burned to death?'

'It is.'

'But how can you be sure? It might only be a rumour.'

'A piece of paper giving this information was smuggled into the village and passed amongst the people. Have you not seen it?'

Léonie shook her head slowly and Madame Renet said, 'Then you must be the only one.' She added, 'Mind you, if I could I would pin it to the wall of this store for all the world to see but I have my business to consider and my skin as well, come to that. If they can do this to the Mayor they can do it to any one of us.'

'Nothing like this has ever happened before,' said Léonie.

'But now it is starting.' Madame Renet lowered her voice and went on, 'Did you know that a bridge was blown up not far from this village and did you not hear that new officials are sitting in the town hall looking for names. Undoubtedly someone has named the Mayor's son and that is why they have burned his father.'

Léonie shook her head sadly. 'He was such a delicate man too. I wonder what will become of his wife?'

'I would not worry about her. She is gone from the village. Besides, she had no time for her husband. It was obvious she thought herself a cut above him because her people were wealthy. He never should have married her.'

'Well, it is all one now,' said Léonie.

The shopkeeper laughed grimly. 'It is for the Mayor.'

Léonie shifted about on the stone floor. Her feet were numb. It was as cold inside the store as it was outside. She said, 'I must be going but thank you for the tobacco. My husband will be pleased.'

As she was leaving Madame Renet called, 'Tonight they are holding a service for the Mayor. Do you think you might come to the church on this occasion?'

'Oh yes,' said Léonie, hurrying away.

At the bottom of the street she encountered Maria Defarge, a large woman with bold, protuberant eyes. She enquired about Léonie's health and without waiting for an answer began to speak excitedly.

'Do you know,' she said, 'last night I dreamed that the town hall was covered in white and from under its door ran a stream of blood. And what do I see when I awake this morning – everything covered in snow. I am positive this is a sign that blood will soon follow.'

They say dreams are only dreams – nothing more,' said Léonie.

'Not my dreams,' said Maria. 'Many times they have come true. I have the gift for seeing signs, as everybody in the village knows.'

'But of course,' said Léonie hurriedly. Maria could cure sores on the face and body as well as other minor ailments. She also cast spells, sometimes for the good and sometimes for the bad. Strangely enough she had never been able to cast spells on the foreign officials.

'It is because they have no souls,' she once explained. 'I can only deal with those who have souls.'

'I hear they are holding a service in church for the Mayor,' Léonie informed her.

'How futile,' said Maria.

'Do you not think it is fitting he should be remembered in some way?'

Maria shrugged. 'We do not need a black crow to remind us.'

'Perhaps not,' said Léonie, aware of Maria's distaste for all matters connected with the church, 'but at least it would be a token of respect.'

'Respect?' said Maria with disgust, and then walked off over the snow with long, purposeful steps as if she was being hounded.

As Léonie recrossed the bridge she saw that the river ran faster and higher than usual. She turned her eyes away from it, but the water roared loud in her ears. Although accepting that the river was a part of nature like a stone or a tree or the earth itself, she had never come to terms with it since the death of her son. It seemed to have a malevolent will of its own. Today it did not concern her so much since her head was filled with the Mayor and the manner of his death. She wished she could get him out of her mind. He was invading it with his sad, inconsolable face.

On arriving home she placed the packet of tobacco carefully on the table. Noticing the fire was almost dead she went outside to fetch logs from the wood-shed and saw Lotz the postman coming down the lane between the house and the shed, his postbag slung over his back.

'Good day,' he said, his face red with cold but still cheerful. Lotz always had been an affable man and the occupation had made him no less affable. He'd even been heard to joke with foreign officials.

'I suppose it could be better,' said Léonie, adding, 'I am surprised you are still delivering.'

'It has taken me much longer today since I am forced to walk.'

Léonie made the observation that it was a wonder there was any mail to deliver with all the restrictions.

'There is always enough to keep me going,' said Lotz.

Léonie told him that apart from government notices she never received any mail at all. Not that she could think of anyone who would write to her except for an aunt who lived in a mountainous region and might be dead for all she knew.

'That is too bad,' said Lotz sympathetically, 'but I do assure you some of the villagers receive mail. There are quite a few letters for the Mayor's wife.'

'So she still lives in her house?'

'I am not sure about that but I deliver them anyway.'

'Perhaps they are letters of condolence?'

'They could very well be,' said Lotz, shaking his head and for once looking serious.

'It is a bad business,' said Léonie. 'One never knows what will happen next.'

'That is true,' said Lotz, hitching his bag farther back on his shoulder. 'We can only carry on the same as usual and hope for the best.' He added, becoming cheerful again, 'I presume you are keeping well yourself?'

'I am always well enough.'

'And your husband?'

'He too is well enough.'

'He is a fine man,' said Lotz. 'He works hard, I'll say that for him.'

'He does,' said Léonie, turning away abruptly to enter the wood-shed.

She kindled the fire and made a loaf with flour and water and prepared a stew with some vegetables then placed both items inside the iron oven that was heated by the fire. After that she went into her son's room in order to feel his presence. It did not come and she was not surprised. It was unreasonable to expect it twice on the same day. In any case, her head was still filled with the Mayor. She was about to leave the room when she felt something standing behind her right shoulder as she sat upon the bed. She knew at once it was the presence of the Mayor. She could hear his breath, harsh and laboured.

'Go away,' she said. 'I have done you no harm.'

It stayed so she called out loudly, 'You cannot stay here. This is my son's room.' Then she added in a moment of inspiration, 'If you leave I will pray for your soul,' and it vanished. She went out of the room thinking she must keep this promise lest the Mayor's presence return and banish that of her son.

A while later she sat at the kitchen table, awaiting her husband's arrival. The bowls and spoons were laid out and the dish of stew simmered on the iron oven. The bread she had baked lay on the dresser, flat and solid. Flour and water alone did not make good bread but it was better than none. Her husband might not think so but at least he should be pacified with the tobacco. When another half-hour passed and he still had not returned she ate some bread and stew, washed her face under the tap in the sink, put on her coat and scarf and set off for the church. Her shoes were still damp but not as damp as they had been.

The grey stone church, diminutive and plain, stood at the highest point of the village. The bells were pealing as Léonie entered. She remembered to dip her fingers in the basin of holy water then cross herself in the direction of the altar before edging into the back pew. Apart from a couple seated near the front the place was empty. They turned round to stare at her. She knew them slightly. Before the occupation they used to sell sweets in the market. She gave them a diffident smile and they turned their heads away, so she leaned back against the wooden partition and studied the walls. Except for a statue of the Virgin in an alcove halfway down the wall, there was nothing to admire. It had not changed since she had come years ago. Perhaps the cracks on the walls and the ceiling had deepened. There was a crack across the face of the Virgin which she did not remember but maybe it had always been there.

More people entered, filling up the empty seats. Two of them sat along from her in the back pew. Léonie waited for the service feeling less alone and more relaxed. When the priest came in from a side door and stood before the altar she leaned forward, listening. His words were indistinct. He was as she remembered him, fairly young, of medium height, his black hair combed back severely from his high forehead. From a distance his complexion looked like the tallow candles on the altar. It dawned on her he was speaking in Latin so she closed her eyes to rest them for a time. When she opened them he was speaking in a normal tongue which she also found difficult to understand as his accent was thick and guttural in the way of those who come from the South. Eventually it became clear that he was condemning certain men who had brought shame and sorrow to the village by their unlawful acts.

At first she thought he was referring to the foreign officials but as he continued it became apparent he was speaking of the men who lived in the mountains.

Now he was saying, 'Those men are lawless and without mercy. They have turned their hearts away from God and do the Devil's work in the guise of saviours. For their own ends they would destroy this village. If it were not for his son, who is one of them, the Mayor would still be alive.'

As he spoke further in this vein there was much coughing and fidgeting from the congregation. For the first time since she had entered the church Léonie noticed Madame Renet in the centre pew. She was speaking openly to her neighbour. The priest was not distracted. He continued

127

to speak out loud and accusingly. He finished his address with the words, ' "Vengeance is mine, saith the Lord," ' then after a pause during which the congregation suddenly became silent, he added more softly, 'Now let us pray for the soul of our Mayor,' and everyone knelt on the praying stool with their hands clasped and heads bowed.

Outside the church Léonie encountered Madame Renet who said, 'It was a very bad service. I am sure the Mayor would not have been pleased with the condemnation of his son and I am certain if his son hears about it he will be even less pleased. I suspect the priest has signed his own death-warrant.'

Léonie replied, 'I am certainly surprised that he spoke out against those men. Though perhaps he thought it his duty to do so in order to prevent bloodshed.'

'He does less than his duty,' said Madame Renet. 'You notice he did not speak out against the enemy. I would not be surprised if he was the one who named the Mayor's son, causing the Mayor to be burned. In fact, after that sermon I am convinced of it. He is nothing more than a traitor.'

'I would not be so sure,' said Léonie.

'Well, I am as sure as the nose on my face.'

'But surely if he was a traitor he would be clever enough to conceal it rather than turn suspicion on himself by giving such a sermon.'

'The priest's pride is colossal. He thinks he is God himself. Apparently he has forgotten the proverb that pride goes before a fall. Mark my words, he will surely soon fall.'

'But nothing is a certainty,' said Léonie, turning away to go in the direction of her house.

★　　　★　　　★

On arriving home she found her husband sitting at the table with his pipe in his hand.

'You have had your meal then?' she said, glancing at the empty stew dish. He did not answer so she took off her coat and scarf and hung them on the peg behind the door then turned back to him saying, 'I waited for you as long as I could.'

But he still sat like a mussel.

She coughed and added, 'This evening I was at the service being held for the Mayor. Lotz's words were true – the Mayor was burned. It's hard to think such a thing could happen.'

'Indeed,' said her husband coldly, filling up his pipe from the packet of tobacco lying on the table.

'At least I managed to get tobacco,' said Léonie somewhat lamely.

When he had filled his pipe and puffed on it for a few seconds he said in a harsh tone, 'You had no right to leave the house at such a late hour without my permission.'

'I thought under the circumstances it was excusable.'

'Under what circumstances?'

'The circumstances of the Mayor's death.'

'So, everything must cease to function because of the Mayor's death?'

'I waited for you so long that I thought you had gone to the bar. Besides, the meal was prepared and the fire was lit. What more could I do?'

'The fire was low and the meal was cold,' said her husband. 'What kind of welcome is that when I come home tired and freezing?'

Léonie bit her lip as she confronted him. His eyes, she noticed, were slightly glazed as though he had been drinking alcohol.

'Then you must have been very late,' she said.

'But not as late as you,' he shouted. He stood up and slapped her face then said, 'Fetch some logs for this fire. It's nearly out and I feel bad enough as it is.'

Léonie touched her burning cheek then went out to fetch logs from the wood-shed, which she put on the fire after first adding some paper. She asked her husband for a match which he flung across in a vicious manner. When the logs began to burn he took his chair over to the fire and sat before it blocking out the heat while Léonie went over and sat with her elbow on the table and chin in hand. Some time passed before her husband turned to her saying, 'In any case, what was the Mayor to you?'

'Nothing,' she said, taking her hand from her chin. 'Why do you ask that?'

'Because you seem to be obsessed with him.'

'I am not obsessed with him. I simply felt sad that he had to die in such a dreadful manner. Any normal person would feel the same.'

'Why do you look so guilty then?'

'Do I?' said Léonie. 'I think it must be your imagination. You have been drinking too much Pernod.'

Her husband stared back at the fire. He appeared to be brooding on something. Léonie began to yawn, not with fatigue, but with nerves. Usually he would fall asleep after his meal but tonight it seemed unlikely. Then he turned to her again.

'I almost forgot to tell you,' he said with a twisted smile.

'The river has burst its banks and my land is covered and the crops are ruined.'

'But that is terrible!' said Léonie, taking her hand from her chin and sitting up straight. 'What will we do?'

'You mean what will *I* do,' said her husband smiling, or at least, baring his teeth for his eyes were cold and glassy.

Léonie whispered, 'Then what will *you* do?'

'Do not worry,' said her husband, 'I have my plans.' He spat into the fire with an air of satisfaction.

Léonie sat blinking with agitation. If the land was covered in water and the crops were ruined they would have no vegetables to eat, and what was worse she would not be rid of him during the day. Her life would become unbearable and although she was consumed with anxiety she felt she dare not question him further, his mood being so irrational. They sat for a good while in silence then without warning he said, 'Tell me, was it the Mayor's son that you once bore?'

Taken aback, Léonie could only stare at him. Then she pulled herself together and said, 'I do not understand you. The Mayor's son is in the mountains, or so I believe.'

'I am speaking of the son you had who was drowned in the river, or have you forgotten about him altogether?'

'What kind of talk is this?' said Léonie. 'It was your son who was drowned in the river or should I say, our son.'

'And yet,' her husband said thoughtfully, 'he never looked like me not by one single feature. I often wondered about that.'

Léonie said as if bewildered, 'If I did not know your land is under water and that you appear to have been drinking

Pernod I would think you have gone out of your mind. As it is I can only feel pity that you are speaking to me like this.'

At that her husband jumped from his seat, gripped her by the shoulders and shook her so hard that when he released her she almost fell on the floor.

'Do not feel pity for me!' he shouted. 'I am a man of some pride and ambition. I will not go under like the other weaklings in this village. I have made my plans.'

Then he returned to his seat at the fire. Léonie sat, faint and trembling. After a long pause she said, 'And what are your plans?'

After a moment's deliberation he said calmly enough, 'I might as well tell you since it will let you know where you stand. My plan is to sell this house and with the money I will begin a new life in another country, where an ambitious man can succeed more easily than he would in this village of incestuous relationships where the Mayor would have any hag who crosses his path, and the priest sleeps with his housekeeper and the occupiers think of us as barbarians and I have no doubt they are right.'

'I see,' said Léonie noticing her husband's eyes were beginning to droop. 'And what of me?'

'And what of you?' he repeated in a tired voice. 'I really do not care. All I know is that I will be encumbered with you no longer. You are not only a stupid woman but an adulteress into the bargain. Even a lesser man than I would not put up with such a wife.'

'I may be stupid but there is no proof I am an adulteress.'

132

'Your look of guilt was proof enough for me,' he muttered, his head bowing with fatigue.

'I see,' said Léonie, clasping her hands tight within her lap. Then she spoke out firmly. 'When I think about your plan it occurs to me it is a good one. I have always had the feeling that this village was no place for a proud and ambitious man like yourself, and now that your land is covered in water and your crops ruined it would seem that the time is ripe for you to leave. In fact I will be very happy if you do so for you may be a proud man but you are a bad husband.'

He gave no sign he heard this so she spoke louder.

'And you were right about the Mayor. Indeed he was a man who would go with any willing female who crossed his path. I should know. I crossed his path quite a few times. Though I am sure the son I bore was yours but that is not important any more since they are both dead. So the sooner you go, the better.'

Still he gave no sign of hearing her and when she looked at him closely she saw he was asleep. She thought how easy it would be to push him into the fire, but the thought passed. Instead she stood up and shook him by the shoulder saying, 'I think it is time you should go to bed.' He lifted his head, stared at her blearily and said, 'Take your hand off me. I am going,' then stumbled over to the bed against the wall and lay down on it fully clothed.

Léonie took over his seat by the fire and stretched her cold hands towards the flames while her husband began to snore. She thought about his plan to leave but somehow had no faith in it. Apart from the accusation about her and the Mayor his words were similar to words she had heard before. She began to conceive a plan of her own. Rising from her seat she went over to the dresser and took from a drawer a sheet of writing paper, a pen and a bottle of ink, all of which had lain there untouched since before the occupation. Then she started to write.

Dear Aunt,

I write to you in the hope that you are keeping well despite these harsh times. In fact I was considering visiting you and perhaps staying with you for a short time or even longer if you wished. I know it cannot be easy for you to manage your small farm so I am willing to help in any way I can and I would not require any payment. As for my keep, I can give you something towards that since I have been saving money in a stocking for this purpose. You see my husband intends to leave the village in order to begin a new life in another place where his ambitions will be better realized. He is a proud man and a hard worker so he is bound to succeed. But since I am not so proud and ambitious I have refused to go with him. On the other hand if you do not find this arrangement suitable please do not hesitate to write and let me know. In any case I will be glad to hear from you since it is a long time since I have had a letter from anyone.

Your affectionate niece,
Léonie.

After addressing the envelope and putting the letter inside it, she entered her son's room and put it under the pillow on his bed. In the dark she undressed then lay between the sheets that were cold but she scarcely noticed this, her mind being so fixed on the letter and the look of surprise which would appear on Lotz's face when she asked him if he would be good enough to post it for her if she gave him money for the stamp. She was so excited by her plan that she forgot to wait for the presence of her son, which did not enter the room at any time during that night.

THE HUT

T he hut was so dark and dreary that I wished we had never come. Hardboard covered the window to keep intruders out, though there was nothing to steal but the spade behind the boiler where we used to light fires. I asked my husband if we should light a fire and he said it wasn't worth it as we wouldn't be stopping long.

'It's all right for you. My feet are freezing.'

'You should have put on something warmer,' he said, which was true, but I hadn't bargained on coming to the hut when we first set out. If I'd known, I would have brought a bottle of sherry like I used to do. On summer evenings we sipped it out of cracked cups while watching the sun go down. That was before he'd had the heart attack.

Everything had been cheerier then. Nowadays we didn't do anything except take the odd short walk if the weather was dry. This was the first time we'd been back for months.

'I wonder what happened to the boy,' I said.

'What boy?'

'The boy who shared the hut with us. He was going to build a pigeon loft and you were supposed to be giving him a hand, remember?'

'Yes, but I don't think he intended building anything. He was too damned lazy. Went about like a half-shut knife, he did.'

'That's not true,' I said indignantly. 'He helped you fix the fence.'

'Only because it suited him.' He lit his pipe for the umpteenth time. I went to the door and gazed out at what had been his vegetable plot. It was covered in grass and weeds and apart from the potato shaws there was no sign of vegetables. Likely they'd been eaten by slugs and rabbits. I turned and asked him if the potatoes were ready for picking.

'They should be. I'll dig them up once I've had a draw.'

I thought he was always having a draw. He said the pipe was less harmful than cigarettes. I suspected he was fooling himself. After a while he lifted the spade and headed for the plot. From the doorway I watched him dig with surprising strength, praying he wouldn't ask me to help him for I couldn't stand the sight of all those beetles crawling over my feet. Then he called on me to bring out some plastic bags. I went inside and looked around the shelves but could see nothing but newspapers.

'Will these do?' I said, stumbling towards him, my shoes covered in mud.

'They'll have to,' he said, then stopped digging to watch me wrap the potatoes. It wasn't easy. They kept falling out.

'Hurry up,' he said, then threw down the spade and said he would have to come back another day because his back was sore.

I arose stiffly, clutching the bundles. When I reached the hut he'd found the plastic bags.

'You couldn't have looked properly,' he said, handing them over. Without a word I transferred the potatoes into the bags then wiped my hands on my coat, noticing that his hands were clean.

'I hope the boy doesn't come back for the spade,' he said, as he was putting it away.

'He's probably got better things to do.'

'Like what?'

'Like enjoying himself.'

'Ah,' he said, as though I'd touched him on a sore point.

It was then I took out a half-smoked cigarette which had been in my coat pocket for ages.

'I thought you'd given them up,' he said. 'You told me you had.'

'So I have. This is the last.'

'Cigarette smoke is bad for my health.'

'Pipe smoke is bad for everybody's health.'

'Nonsense. It's a different type of smoke altogether.' There was no point in arguing. The cigarette tasted foul but gave me the courage to tell him that if he didn't light a fire I was going home.

'All right,' he said, 'but don't blame me if the wood is too damp.'

I thought, he must be cold himself when he did as I suggested. The wood caught fire and soon flames were licking the edge of the boiler. In a better mood I said I'd like to do a sketch of the hut one day. It would be something to look back on if it was ever dismantled. He studied me narrowly.

'I recollect you saying that once before.'

'When was that?'

'One evening last summer when the boy was here. It seemed to amuse him. He laughed at you.'

'I don't remember,' I said hotly.

'Likely because you'd drunk too much sherry. I know I had a few myself but it was no excuse for his attitude.'

'What attitude?'

'He was forever interrupting me when I spoke and I caught him staring at you when he thought I wasn't looking. I don't know what would have happened if I hadn't been there.'

'For God's sake, he was only a boy –' I began, then broke off. My husband was a sick man. I'd better not say anything to put his blood-pressure up.

'I believe that's the rain on,' I said, hearing it patter on the roof. 'It's a good job you got the potatoes in when you did.'

'Yes,' he said vaguely, as though his mind was elsewhere.

A gust of wind blew the door open. As I closed it I saw the sky had turned black. When it was closed we could hardly see a thing.

'We'll have to make a run for it before the rain gets any heavier,' I said.

'I'm in no shape to run. Look on the shelf. There should be a candle in that empty sherry bottle.'

142

I felt along the shelf and found the bottle. There was hardly any candle left but I put a match to it while my husband puffed on his pipe. The smoke made me cough.

'I'll have to get out of here,' I said. 'I feel as though I'm choking.'

'Do what you like.'

Angered by the way he spoke and now not giving a damn about his blood-pressure, I asked what he thought the boy would have done if he hadn't been there. He stroked his chin then finally said, 'Something diabolic no doubt.'

When I told him to be more precise he said, 'The state you were in he could have stolen your purse.'

'I didn't have a purse with me.'

'Oh well,' he shrugged, 'I'm sure he would have done something objectionable. He was that type of boy.'

'You know what I think?' I said. 'I think you were jealous of him. That's why you're running him down.'

'Me, jealous of him?' he sneered. 'Don't make me laugh.'

'All right, I won't,' I said, 'but it seems strange to me when I've always found the boy helpful and obliging. His only fault, if you could call it that, was a tendency to blush, which I suppose would irritate someone like you whose skin is as thick as putty.'

As a final thrust I said the boy reminded me of my son.

'What son?'

'The son I would have had but for the miscarriage.'

He stared at me wildly. 'You're not going to bring that up, are you?'

'Why shouldn't I?' I said, staring defiantly back. Then the candle went out and we were in the dark.

'Aren't you going to say something?' I said, after a long pause.

'About what?'

'About the boy.'

'Certainly not.'

I wasn't surprised. He would be offended now. I was never allowed to mention the miscarriage. It was like a crime that had to be kept hidden. Driven by this bitter reflection, I added daringly, 'Come to think of it, our son might have turned out like the boy, both in nature and looks. Did you ever think of that?'

He groaned. 'I'll try my best not to.'

'Especially when you've got your blood-pressure to think of.'

I wondered if I'd gone too far when I saw him lift the spade from behind the boiler.

'What are you doing?' I asked.

'I'm taking this home in case it gets stolen. I'll need it for the rest of the potatoes.'

'I suppose you could,' I said, relieved but thinking him an idiot to attach so much importance to a spade. 'I won't be coming back with you. It's depressing enough without having to sit around a dark, freezing hut.'

'Suit yourself,' he said in his usual irritable tone. Then he stood up and opened the door. 'The rain's off.' Sure enough when I looked out the sky had cleared and the sun was shining brightly on the puddles.

'Right, let's go,' he said. 'You bring the potatoes and I'll take the spade.'

'Aren't you going to lock the door?' I asked him as he was walking away.

He thought for a minute then said, 'I might as well leave it open for that dratted boy. Knowing him, he's likely lost his own key. That's probably why he hasn't been back.'

'Yes, you'd better,' I said, 'since you've just stolen his spade.'

'I'm not stealing it. He'll get it back when I see him.'

I thought that could be never, but I merely answered, 'We might even have managed to buy one of our own by then.'

THE CASTLE

It had been a long journey. Twenty-four hours it had taken because we had come the cheapest way possible: first by train and boat, then train again and finally a tedious two hours by bus. The hotel room, booked for us by the Continental Travel Agency, was small and cramped but otherwise clean. Somewhat dazed I stared over the balcony outside the window. My sister Mary Jane squeezed into the rail beside me.

'This isn't bad at all,' she said. 'What do you think?'

'Where's the sea?' I asked. The holiday brochure had said that the village was close to the Mediterranean but we appeared to be in a valley – white cliffs on one side, rolling hills on the other and, facing us in the distance, a range of shadowy mountains.

'It can't be far,' said Mary Jane, swivelling her head. 'Isn't that a castle on top of the cliff?'

'Where?' I asked, but now she was pointing to the courtyard.

'Look at that fountain, all gushing with water! And those apartments over by the river with their balconies and shutters. It's just how I imagined a French village would be – and all this lovely heat too. That's what I miss most about India – the heat.

'It is warm,' I said, wiping my clammy forehead, 'but you'd have thought there would be more people about.' Down below, the square was deserted apart from one old woman in dark clothes shuffling along the pavement with a bundle of sticks under her arm. 'Isn't this place supposed to a popular tourist attraction?'

'The tourist season will be over by now. And I think it's perfect the way it is, slow moving and tranquil and all this sun. What more could one ask for?'

When I looked back at the small bedroom, barely big enough for one, I wished we'd asked for separate rooms, but the booking had been done at the last minute, and it was probably too late now. I supposed it was all very nice but I was too hot and tired to appreciate it. Mary Jane suggested that after lunch we take a stroll by the river.

'Actually I was thinking of having a rest afterwards,' I said.

'A rest?' she said incredulously. 'On the first day of our holiday?'

'But I'm tired. It would only be an hour at the most.'

'Honest to God, Dorothy – didn't you have enough sleep on the bus?' She went on to say that she hoped I wasn't going to spoil everything by being tired all the time for in that case I should have stayed at home. I thought that was a good one. She knew I hadn't wanted to come – but she'd harped on so much about it that I'd finally given in.

'We might never get another chance at our age,' she'd said at the time, mentioning Father as a example of how easily one could go into a decline.

It never seemed to occur to Mary Jane to worry about money. Ever since she came home from abroad after Father died – only for a visit, she said, but that was two years ago – she'd been spending it like water. Nor did it occur to her that half-shares might be a bit unfair when I was the one who stayed at home to care for him while she went gallivanting all over the world 'having a wonderful time', as she said on her postcards. It was hard not to be bitter at times, but I tried to put the past out of my mind. There was the future to consider. She was saying, 'After all, you're only fifty-six, just two years older than me, and look at you – fat as a pudding. It's exercise you need, not a rest.'

'I'll see how I feel later,' I said, thinking I'd rather be fat as a pudding than thin as a rake like her.

Lunch was served in the restaurant downstairs by the proprietor – a Monsieur Savlon whom we'd met briefly when we arrived. Though weary I had been struck by his singular appearance. He was almost as short as he was broad and without a single hair on his head. As if to make up for this his beard grew very thick and black. The meal he laid before us was heavy with sauce and the predominant flavour was garlic, which I cannot stand. I left half of it on my plate and drank almost a jugful of water to get rid of the taste. When Monsieur Savlon came back to clear the table he asked me in perfectly good English, 'You do not like snails?' I shook my head and hurried off to the toilet where I was violently sick. Fifteen minutes later Mary Jane came up to the room and found me lying on top of the bed.

'You really are the limit,' she said. 'Don't you know snails are a delicacy?'

'I don't want to know anything,' I said, turning on my side and closing my eyes.

The next thing I knew she was towering above me in a long white cotton night-dress. 'What time is it?' I asked, for one horrible moment thinking it was Father. For the last few years before he died he had worn a night-shirt that looked much the same.

'You may well ask,' she said, the freckles on her face standing out like halfpence pieces. 'You've been asleep for almost a day. I don't know how often I tried to wake you but you simply refused. I was really fed up. And on top of that Monsieur Savlon kept asking about you. I didn't know what to say.'

'I'm sorry,' I said, forcing myself off the bed. I went out onto the balcony where the air was pleasantly cool. A mist hung over the river. The streets and the apartments looked fresh and sparkling. There was that air of quiet expectancy about the place you get first thing on a fine morning. I began to feel remarkably well.

'Let's go out as soon as we've had breakfast,' I suggested, 'and see as much as we can before it gets too hot. We could even take a picnic to save us coming back for lunch. I'm sure Monsieur Savlon wouldn't mind.'

Mary Jane frowned. 'I hope you don't expect me to run around like a mad thing just because you've had a good rest. I haven't unpacked my things yet and I'll have to think about what to wear. I hate being rushed.'

I stifled a sigh. 'All right, we won't rush.'

In the restaurant Monsieur Savlon came over with a pot

of coffee and a plate piled high with toast. 'You like?' he asked, his hands wavering over jars of honey, marmalade and jam. I nodded my head earnestly to wipe out any bad impressions I had given him previously.

'You want more?'

'No thanks,' said Mary Jane.

'This looks very appetizing,' I said, and flushed, for no good reason I could think of.

'What a fussy little man he is,' said Mary Jane.

'He's only doing his best to please us,' I said, biting into a slice of toast and honey. When my plate was clean I asked her if she would mind telling him when she got the chance that I couldn't stand snails or garlic, but that this was no reflection on his excellent cooking.

'Tell him yourself,' she said.

'It doesn't matter,' I said, for I didn't want to admit that I sometimes feel shy with foreigners. I knew she would only jeer.

Mary Jane took a long time unpacking. Then she couldn't decide what to wear. 'So you think I should put this on?' she said, holding up a dark-blue dress which she had brought back from India, of a material so fine that it was almost transparent.

'Why not?' I said. 'It looks cool.'

She studied it, frowning. Then she shoved it back into the wardrobe. 'It's not casual enough for walking,' she complained. 'Anyone can see that.' Finally she settled for a pair of shorts and a T-shirt, saying that she might as well be comfortable. I thought that her thin white legs would have been better covered up but there was no point in saying so, for she'd always go against anything I suggested.

All the same, I began to feel overdressed in my skirt and blouse, so as a gesture of freedom I took off my tights. We were a few yards away from the hotel when I remembered that I'd forgotten to ask Monsieur Savlon for a picnic basket. I didn't mention this, however, for Mary Jane would have insisted on turning back and with the sun out in full force I was already too hot to be bothered. As we were passing the fountain Mary Jane brought a camera out of her bag and took a snapshot of water gushing from a lion's mouth into a basin floating with dead leaves.

'What's so special about that?' I asked.

'It will look splendid when it's enlarged and framed,' she said, looking at me pityingly. 'I do know what I'm talking about when it comes to photography.'

When we were walking over the bridge Mary Jane stopped to take a shot of a woman on the other side of the road who was dragging a child along by the hand. When the woman began to shout angrily I hurried ahead. 'You shouldn't do that to people,' I said, when Mary Jane caught up with me. 'If you want to take photos of people we can take each other's.' I turned down some steps which led onto the river-bank.

'It's characterization I want, not stodgy snaps of each other. Anyway, where are we going? I never said I wanted to go this way.'

'I thought you wanted to walk by the river.'

'I wanted to go to the castle,' she said huffily, shoving the camera back into her bag as if she had no further use for it, 'but it seems I've no choice.'

When we reached a spot shaded by trees I said that

154

I would have to sit down since my new sandals were rubbing.

'Oh no!' she groaned.

'But look,' I said, undoing the straps and showing her my heels which were blistered and bleeding.

'You should have kept on your tights,' she said. 'What do we do now – go back?' She gave a hollow laugh and lay down on the grass with her hands behind her head. I could have wept with vexation at this point but I knew it would be a mistake. Mary Jane has a cruel streak that thrives on my tears.

'What's wrong with staying here?' I said. 'It's cool and pleasant. At least we're outside.'

'I'm bored' said Mary Jane. 'That's what's wrong. And anyway, you forgot to bring the picnic basket, didn't you?'

The lunch was good – cold salmon and salad. 'No garlic,' said Monsieur Savlon with a twinkle in his eye.

I wondered how he knew about the garlic. Perhaps Mary Jane had told him after all. She was in a good mood now, smiling broadly as she clutched her glass of wine. She had ordered a bottle which I thought was far too much for so early in the day. By the time we had finished the meal more diners had arrived. I was glad for Monsieur Savlon's sake because until now trade had been poor. After lunch Mary Jane offered to go into the village to buy some Elastoplast for my heels. I told her I'd be very grateful; at the same time I wondered how she was going to manage this, for she must have put away four or five glasses of wine by now.

As I watched her leave I noticed that she was walking

very straight. Too straight, I thought. An hour later she came back and told me that she'd been wandering round the village and had seen some wonderful sights. There was one street in particular, she said enthusiastically, that had the most amazing houses – all different shapes and sizes with cute little courtyards filled with the most amazing flowers and plants. What a pity I hadn't been with her. Then she gave a large yawn and slumped into the chair.

'Did you remember the Elastoplast?' I asked.

'Goodness,' she said, 'I completely forgot.'

Dinner that evening was an excellent steak followed by a soufflé so light that it melted on the tongue. Mary Jane, however, sat drowsily throughout the meal and eventually said she'd have to have an early night since the heat had completely worn her out. Much later I sat out on the balcony in the dark. There was nothing to see except the reflections of the bridge and the apartments cast upon the river by the street lamps. Behind me Mary Jane lay snoring.

I looked at my watch. It was only half-past nine.

The next morning when we were up and dressed Mary Jane said, 'Let's do something exciting. This is our third day and we've done nothing at all.'

'What do you suggest?'

'I was thinking about the castle.'

I pulled open the shutters. There was no cool morning mist – only the sun blinding my eyes. 'It's too hot for climbing,' I said.

'It won't get any cooler. This is the South of France, you know.'

'I'd never get up that cliff,' I protested.

'Don't be stupid. You don't go straight up the cliff. There's a path at the side. Monsieur Savlon told me.'

'Can't we leave it for another day? We've got plenty of time. We don't have to do everything all at once, surely?'

This threw her into a rage. 'We've done hardly anything,' she shouted. 'Honest to God, I wish I'd never come on this holiday. I can see it's going to be a right disaster.'

Suddenly I was infuriated by everything: the heat, this sombre village and most of all by Mary Jane. Things always had to go her way and that's what it had been like ever since she'd moved in. 'And I wish you'd never come to live with me in the first place,' I shouted back. Mary Jane's eyes narrowed and her mouth tightened ominously. I began to regret my words. I was afraid that she might start throwing things around the room and I didn't want Monsieur Savlon at the door.

'I'm sorry,' I said quickly. 'I didn't mean it. The words just slipped out.'

'You meant it, all right,' she said, storming out of the bedroom and banging the door behind her.

I followed her into the toilet and said that I was sorry, I'd spoken in a temper because I'd had a bad headache all morning, but if she was really set on going to the castle I would go with her. The main thing was for us not to fall out over trifles.

'Trifles?' she repeated, staring at me oddly in the mirror above the wash basin. 'So Father was right about you after all.'

'What do you mean?' I demanded.

'As a matter of fact, Father wrote to me not long before

he died, saying that you had terrible bouts of temper. He complained that you weren't the loving, patient Dorothy he used to know. In fact, the poor thing even suspected that you were trying to poison him. He said he caught you putting something in his tea one night.'

'But he always drank cocoa,' I said, bemused.

'Anyway, by the time I arrived home he was already dead. So I decided it was best to let sleeping dogs lie, if you'll pardon the expression.'

I stared at her, outraged. Mary Jane would say anything to spite me, but to more or less accuse me of trying to poison Father was going a bit far even for her.

'I gave him a tranquillizer every night to make him sleep. He died of a heart attack. It was on the certificate.'

'I don't doubt it was, but doctors can be careless.' She paused for a minute then added defensively, 'I'm only saying what he wrote.'

Mary Jane was an atrocious liar, I knew that. I wondered if there had ever been a letter at all. Before Father died he had still been able to totter around, but I could hardly imagine him going out to buy a stamp.

'So if he thought I was poisoning him why didn't he cut me out of his will?'

Mary Jane gave a shrug. 'I'd never have mentioned it in the first place if you hadn't been so hurtful,' she said sulkily.

We were about to leave the hotel and head for the castle when Monsieur Savlon came running after us to tell us it was going to rain. Overhead the sky was monotonously blue as ever.

'It can't,' said Mary Jane.

'It says on forecast it will rain.'

'Forecasts aren't always right,' Mary Jane snapped, and left him on the doorstep shaking his head.

We crossed the bridge and had just turned right into a narrow street which Mary Jane said should take us to the bottom of the cliff, when the sky darkened. A minute later it began to pour. In two seconds we were soaked through as we ran back to the café on the corner.

Men were playing cards around a table in the centre of the room, and behind the counter a very fat woman stood regarding us with a mixture of hostility and surprise.

'This doesn't look much like a café,' I said.

'I'll see what they've got,' said Mary Jane, going to the bar, while I dumped our bags on a table beside a window which was covered with wire mesh.

Mary Jane came back to the table with two glasses of milky-looking stuff which according to her was all they sold, unless I preferred beer, of course.

'What is it?' I asked. 'Are you sure they don't have coffee?'

'Pernod,' she said. 'I was told they haven't.' She took a sip from the glass. 'It's not bad. Why don't you try it? It might take the miserable look off your face.'

'I'm not drinking that,' I said, feeling very agitated, because the card players were staring across at us intently. When one of them winked and jerked his head over his shoulder as if to suggest that we join them I said to Mary Jane that we had better leave.

'Can't you take a joke?' Mary Jane began, but I was already on my feet and heading for the door with my bag in hand. Outside it was still raining but not so heavily. I made my way as fast as I could back to the hotel, and although I turned round once or twice to see if Mary Jane was following me, there was no sign of her.

Up in the room I took off my wet clothes and lay down under the bedcovers in my underslip, wondering whether to pack my bags straightaway or wait until tomorrow. The holiday was turning out much worse than I had anticipated. If the past three days were anything to go by there was no likelihood of it getting any better. In the end I gave up trying to work out what to do and fell asleep through sheer inertia.

'Madame, are you there?' Monsieur Savlon was shouting through the keyhole.

I sat up, startled. 'Yes. What is it?'

'Your sister is in the bar. I think she has too much to drink. She is lying on the floor.'

'I'll be down in a minute,' I called, but as soon as I heard his footsteps receding down the stairs I jumped out of bed and locked the door. As far as I was concerned Mary Jane could stay where she was. Right at this moment it was quite beyond me to cope with her.

Prompt on six o'clock I went into the restaurant, for the sandwiches in my bag were damp and soggy and I hadn't eaten since breakfast. There were a few other diners in the room but Mary Jane wasn't among them. I sat down at our usual table anticipating some sharp words from Monsieur Savlon; if he ordered us out it would solve the problem of whether to leave or not, but I dreaded having to face him all the same. However, he laid a bowl of soup in front of me and said quickly, 'Your sister, she is sleeping in my mother's room. Do not worry. She will be fine.' Before I could thank him for his trouble he went on, 'Tonight I plan something special for you. I think you will like.' I looked up at him blankly. Hesitating, he added, 'Perhaps if Madame wears the nice dress she has on when she arrive it would be suitable for this plan.' Then without waiting for an answer, he disappeared into the kitchen.

Upstairs I searched for the dress he had mentioned and found it lying creased on the wardrobe floor. Anyway, what did it matter, I thought, since I wasn't going anywhere. If it was a surprise-party he was talking about, I didn't want any surprises. I would only feel awkward. I wouldn't be able to speak to anyone and I could envisage Mary Jane showing up drunk and making a spectacle of herself. I sat out on the balcony staring at the reflections on the river, wondering angrily if this was what I had come to France for. When I went back into the room, the wardrobe door was still open, and my eye fell on the dark-blue dress that Mary Jane had brought back from India. I tried it on and it fitted me rather well. The cloth had been cut in such a way that it flared out under the high bodice, flattering my full figure. As I studied myself in the wardrobe mirror I decided that I'd never looked so elegant, and that I would go to this affair after all, if only to show my face.

There was no one in the bar except Monsieur Savlon and the tiny old woman who collected the tumblers from the tables on the terrace.

'Am I too early?' I asked. It was nine o'clock. I'd imagined everything would have been in full swing by now.

'*Non, non* – you sit here,' said Monsieur Savlon, pointing to a table in the centre of the room. All the others had been stacked against the wall to clear a space on the floor. 'You will take some?' he said, opening a bottle of wine. 'Very good. Very old.' I sipped the wine, scarcely tasting it, as he sat down opposite me. 'I drink this only on my birthday,' he said.

'I see,' I said. 'You're having a birthday party?'

He frowned as if he did not quite understand. 'I celebrate with you.'

'How thoughtful,' I said faintly, as I caught the eye of the old woman, who stood watching behind the bar counter, nodding her head slightly as if in approval.

'You like music?' asked Monsieur Savlon.

'Yes, I do.'

'Then my mother will play.' He snapped his fingers at the counter, and as if a switch had been pressed the sound of violins filled the room. It struck me as all rather weird – the music, the absence of guests and in particular the fact that this small shabby woman was Monsieur Savlon's mother. I must say I would have expected someone more grand.

'You want to dance now?' he asked.

It was the last thing I wanted to do. I hadn't danced since my school-days, when we had all been forced to take lessons, but I couldn't very well refuse him. As it happened, Monsieur was an excellent dancer, which made it easy for me to follow his lead, and I began to enjoy myself exceedingly.

'The music is called "La Vie en rose",' he said when he led me back to the table. Time passed quickly after that. We danced, then stopped to rest and sip our wine, savouring it slowly as befits a good one. After we had danced for about the sixth time – although I had lost count, really – Monsieur Savlon looked at his watch and said, 'We will now finish. It is late.' He called out to his mother, who had not moved an inch from her position behind the counter, and the violins played no more. I thanked Monsieur Savlon for a pleasant evening, but when I turned to thank his mother she had gone, and it was with a pang of sadness that I climbed the stairs, for it seemed unlikely that such an evening would ever come my way again.

Mary Jane was sitting up in bed when I entered the room.

'Where the hell have you been?' she asked, in a voice sharp as tempered steel. 'And what are you doing with my dress on?'

I explained that I had only been trying on the dress to see how it looked, and had forgotten to take it off when I went downstairs to the bar to look for her.

'You're lying,' she said. 'When I went down to the bar the door was locked. What's more, I could hear music.' I felt my face flushing as she squinted at me curiously. Then her eyes went wide with dawning realization. 'Don't tell me you were having it off with that old dwarf! My God, you must be desperate.'

Next morning Mary Jane told me that she was going to have another try at the castle. 'Do you want to come along?' she asked, pointing out that it wasn't as hot as before.

'I might as well,' I muttered, finding it difficult to look her in the face – particularly since at that very moment

Monsieur Savlon put the coffee pot on the table with his usual brisk 'Good morning'. After he had gone Mary Jane leaned across the table and whispered, 'Mind you, he might not be such a bad catch when you think about it. Must be worth a mint.'

An hour later we were out in the middle of a field which had more stones than grass in it. Mary Jane was walking on ahead while I lagged behind, trying to keep a good distance between us.

'I've found the path,' she shouted. 'Do hurry up.' When I caught up with her she was sitting on a flat stone, looking up at a rough track which led over baked earth and rock to the castle above.

'What do you think?' she asked.

'I think I'll manage,' I replied.

We began to climb. The path itself wasn't so terribly steep, but the effort of side-stepping over loose boulders tired me out. Mary Jane was always ahead, but not by much, and I was only minutes behind her when I reached the top.

'So you finally made it,' she said, as I stood there breathless, looking around for somewhere to rest my aching legs. 'There it is.' She pointed towards a heap of ruins at the edge of the cliff. She set off towards it, camera in hand, while I followed reluctantly. From close up, all that remained of the castle was a long, narrow enclosure of stonework. Grass and flowers grew through the smashed flagstones, and the rampart wall on the edge of the cliff was broken in parts.

'That looks dangerous,' I said, but Mary Jane wasn't listening. She was too busy focusing the camera on the scene, aiming it this way and that, as if what she was doing was all so terribly important. I might have been amused at her antics if I hadn't been so busy watching where she put her feet.

'How about one of you?' she said, pointing the camera in my direction.

'Some other time. I'm not in the mood.'

'You never are in the mood,' she said. She gave an ugly laugh. 'Except if it's Monsieur Savlon, of course.'

'Don't start that again,' I said. I walked away from her and looked over the parapet wall. It was a sheer drop down to the river below. Mary Jane came to stand beside me.

'Magnificent, isn't it? You can see everything for miles around.'

I stepped back. My head was beginning to spin. 'I must have a drink of water,' I said, turning back into the enclosure. We sat on two flat stones and drank from our flasks without looking at each other.

'I've been thinking things over,' Mary Jane said, 'and I might as well tell you I've decided to go back to India. I had a letter from Lady Bonham Fletcher and apparently she misses me terribly and is desperate to have me back. I wasn't going to go because I didn't want to leave you on your own, but the way things are going . . .' She let her voice tail off, as if there were no need for further explanation.

'Why don't you?' I said. Knowing what a liar she was, I was positive she had no intention of going to India. 'I'm sure it's the best thing you could do.'

'So we'll have to sell the house,' she added.

'What do you mean – sell the house?'

'It's plain enough. I'm entitled to half of Father's estate

and if I'm leaving the country the only way I can get it is for us to sell the house.'

'Mary Jane,' I said, 'please stop all this nonsense. I know you don't mean a word of it.'

'Oh, but I do,' she broke in. 'I want the house sold. It's as simple as that. And anyway,' she went on, 'you've got to admit it's in a terrible state – all that old piping and the place is rotten with damp. Just think, with your share you could buy yourself a nice little flat. It would be so much cheaper to run and easier to clean.'

My throat had gone dry. I began to trace circles in the dust with my finger. Mary Jane stared at me stonily. 'Aren't you going to say anything? You've got to face facts, you know. You've really no option.'

'Perhaps you're right,' I said at last. 'I might be better off in a small flat. I can't say I'd considered it before, but if you say you're going back to India . . .'

'Of course I'm right,' she said with such obvious relief that I didn't know whether to laugh or cry. 'Well now,' she went on cheerfully, 'I must take a photo of you in front of the castle. Something to look back on.'

It turned out that there was too much shade there for the camera, and Mary Jane moved me on. 'I'll take it over by the wall,' she said. 'It's brighter there.' After a bit of manoeuvring to get the exact focus, she clicked the shutter. 'That's it,' she said. 'Now you can take one of me.'

'By the wall?'

'Of course, by the wall.' Mary Jane took up a pose with one arm arranged on top of the wall.

'Move over a bit,' I said. 'You're too far to the left.'

'For goodness sake,' she said irritably. Fixing her smile on the camera, she took a step sideways. Then her arm flailed in empty space and she went backwards through the gap without uttering a word of protest.

Mary Jane was buried in the village cemetery. The coroner's verdict was accidental death. Monsieur Savlon came to the funeral along with a few of the old village women, including his mother. It was a simple affair. The coffin was placed inside a marble tombstone and a priest said a few brief words. As I was leaving the cemetery Monsieur Savlon came up to offer his condolences. 'Be patient, Madame,' he said. 'Time will heal your pain.'

Personally I thought I'd been patient long enough. Through my tears I told him that it would have been some consolation to visit my sister's grave at least once a week, but alas, I couldn't even do that. Monsieur Savlon stopped and confronted me. 'But why not? You can stay for as long as you want – for ever, if you wish.'

'For ever?' I said with astonishment.

'Forgive me,' he said. 'I have offended you perhaps. It is not the right time to say this.'

'I'll think about it,' I said, turning away and wiping my eyes.

I am taking up Monsieur Savlon's offer. It's the best thing that could have happened. He has told me that there's an empty apartment across the river. He knows the owner very well and he's sure that I can get it. He assures me that the rent won't be too dear, since it's a poor village and no one is expected to pay more than they can afford. I can scarcely get over my good luck. After all those years of stagnating in Father's old house, I'm about to live in an apartment in a French village with a balcony overlooking the river. Of course I'm sad about Mary Jane, in a way. But she was her own worst enemy. Which reminds me – I must get rid of her writing bureau before I sell the house. That's where she kept all her correspondence, and as she said herself, it's better to let sleeping dogs lie. I still can't help feeling angry, though, when I think of her calling Monsieur Savlon a dwarf. How dare she say that about such a nice little man.

MARCHING TO THE HIGHLANDS
AND INTO THE UNKNOWN

In June 1949 my first husband, baby daughter of two months, and myself set forth for the North of Scotland. This venture was prompted by an article in a paper saying that people were wanted to work land in the Highlands, with accommodation provided. I was not keen on marching into the unknown, but it was a case of squaw follows Indian brave and asks no questions. So with £11, our baby, our clothing, a two-man tent and pram we took the train from Glasgow to a station beyond Inverness called Garve. It dawned on me then that we had no idea where we were going, apart from a vague intention to reach a place called Scoraig situated on the Little Minch.

I remember we obtained a lift from a tradesman going in the direction of Scoraig, but he had heard nothing about work and accommodation. We arrived at Scoraig and the only sign of habitation was a single house staring from a high point towards the Atlantic Sea. We might as well have been in the Sahara. We spied a small brick building, possibly a shelter for animals, and inside this we huddled, hating each other, while I attempted to feed the baby. However, a woman came down from the house and took us in and gave us a room to sleep in. She must have thought us mad, but accepted our story and for a week we camped in her garden. Her husband, who worked on the road, told us it was the only work available. The only payment we could give her, though she wanted none, was a carton of Epsom salts. She was as grateful as if we had given her a magnificent gift. We promised to write when we were in better circumstances. Sadly, we never did.

We set off back through this mountainous region, possibly beautiful if you were a tourist, but to me desolate and harsh, gushing rivers and jagged rocks.

We came to an inn stuck in the middle of nowhere and, overjoyed at this bit of civilization, set up our tent beside it. The buxom woman who owned the place sold us food, even offering my husband a job. She took a fancy to him but not to me.

After two days of camping and happiness for my husband, mainly because of his access to beer, I took the initiative and unpegged the tent, wrapped it up, and we set off again in silence. I can't remember how long it took us to reach the town of Beauly but by the end of the journey we were both covered in cleg bites. The baby in her pram was protected by wet nappies hanging over the hood. The money was nearly gone. In Beauly I located what nowadays would be called a social security office and managed to obtain 14s by genuinely sobbing my heart out and holding the baby who cried too. This allowed us to buy food and walk to Inverness.

We reached Inverness and put up the tent in a place called, I think, The Black Park Camping Site, for a few shillings weekly. We stayed here for quite a while, since my husband got a job to do with erecting pylons. It couldn't have been much fun for him going to work from a tent but I had problems too, walking every day from the site to the town for a few herrings or whatever was cheap, and making food on the Primus stove which was difficult to light. I remember one occasion when my husband complained about his meal and I threw the semolina for the baby round the tent in a fit of temper. On another I nearly set the tent on fire in the night while heating milk for the baby.

And yet there were occasions when I was happy pushing the pram along the canal bank or sitting by the river. It was summer and the place was lovely. This situation continued until late September when the weather became colder and the days shorter.

About this time I decided I could not carry on living in a tent with an infant a few months old and the winter approaching. One Saturday evening I packed and, pushing the pram, headed for Inverness railway station to return home to my mother. I left my husband in the tent drinking whisky.

I had to wait some time for the Glasgow train and, before it came, I turned about and pushed the pram back to the tent and that was that. We both decided to leave. We now had some money from my husband's work so a few days later we assembled our belongings and we left Inverness on a train for Keith, another destination unknown to us. Anywhere, we thought then, was better than returning to Glasgow.

We arrived in Keith in the dark, came to a field and pulled our tent round about us. We marched through the town the next morning, not a big place then as I remember it. We purchased some groceries from a shop in the town square owned by a man called McGillviray who asked us questions – why and where and what were we doing. We answered shamefacedly. 'There's a man lives here, originally from Glasgow,' he said. 'I'm sure he'll let you put your tent up in his back garden, it's a good size.'

This man called Alec Simpson did just that and his wife washed our grimy clothes and the baby's nappies. Alec was pleased with us because my husband came from Glasgow and I had worked there. For a fortnight we camped in his back garden, burning fires at night, hanging our clothes to dry over the fence. The townsfolk called us the squatters. Before October ended we moved to a broken-down old building.

We lived there for a year. We were comfortable. We had coal, paraffin light, and my husband got a job with the English Electric Company. My second child, a boy, was born in Keith hospital. We might have lived in Keith for ever but the woman who owned the condemned building told us regretfully that it was being knocked down and we must leave. It was then my husband and I parted for a time. I returned to my home town and he went on working with English Electric. I've often wished to go back to Keith and see it all again, but no doubt everything would be unrecognizable now.

This adventure was judged by a councillor in my home town as 'irresponsible' – I was desperately applying to him for one of the available prefabricated houses. We got the prefab after waiting another year and a half and my husband and I, plus another son and daughter making four children in all, lived not particularly happily ever after until he died at the age of forty-three.

I suppose you could say my life was a struggle, as it is with most men and women of the working class even in years of good employment. I always worked when possible at anything I could find, i.e., in shop, office and factory. That was in the good old days when work brought satisfaction even if it was a hassle. Work was money and security and if I was not exactly happy with my lot I could relax with a drink at the weekend while watching the telly. Any disagreement which arose under the influence was forgotten when facing work on Monday. Yet I suppose there was always a hankering to do something better.

Twelve years ago I began writing fiction, prompted by the fact that I had joined a writing class in Alexandria. Glasgow University sent tutors, who were enthusiastic about what I wrote. When they stopped attending the class I simply carried on writing and periodically some of them got in touch as if to prod me on with that lonely business. Sometimes it was the last thing I wanted to do, especially after cleaning somebody's house, which was now the only job I could get. The years of unemployment had set in.

Then my novel *Gentlemen of the West* was published and some short stories in a book, shared with two other authors, called *Lean Tales*. This was great but didn't pay the rent, so I continued to clean houses and, with the assistance of a grant from the Scottish Arts Council, wrote another short novel called *Like Birds in the Wilderness*. It wasn't a success though some people liked it.

Eight years later, Bloomsbury published *A Working Mother* and now I have completed this collection of stories. Since the depression of the past decade took the security of steady work away from my present husband Patrick, from myself and from countless others, I am thankful to be still in the business of writing. At least I can tell my grandchildren (if they are interested) that not only did I publish a few books in my time but I once was 'irresponsible' enough to set off with my first husband and child into the unknown wilds of the Scottish Highlands where we wandered about with scarcely a penny in our pockets.

A NOTE ON THE AUTHOR

Agnes Owens is the author of *Gentlemen of the West*, *Lean Tales* (with James Kelman and Alasdair Gray), *Like Birds in the Wilderness* and *A Working Mother*. She lives in Scotland.